HARRY LIPKIN, PRIVATE EYE

HARRY LIPKIN,

· PRIVATE EYE ·

BARRY FANTONI

Doubleday

New York London Toronto

Sydney Auckland

Copyright © 2012 by Barry Fantoni

All rights reserved. Published in the United States by Doubleday, a division of Random House, Inc., New York. Originally published in Great Britain by Polygon, an imprint of Birlinn Limited.

www.doubleday.com

DOUBLEDAY and the portrayal of an anchor with a dolphin are registered trademarks of Random House, Inc.

Jacket design by Michael J. Windsor

LIBRARY OF CONGRESS CATALOGING-IN-PUBLICATION DATA
Fantoni, Barry.
Harry Lipkin, private eye / Barry Fantoni. —1st ed.
p. cm.
1. Older men—Fiction. 2. Private investigators—Florida—
Fiction. 3. Miami (Fla.)—Fiction. I. Title.
PR6056.A59H37 2012
823'.914—dc23
2011043572

ISBN 978-0-385-53610-3

MANUFACTURED IN THE UNITED STATES OF AMERICA

10 9 8 7 6 5 4 3 2 1

First United States Edition

For Maxie and The Nightingale

HARRY LIPKIN, PRIVATE EYE

Harry Introduces Himself

Harry Lipkin. Eighty-seven. Eighty-eight next birthday. You think that's old? My mother lived to be a hundred and three. So. Make a note. Send Harry Lipkin a card and a box of soft candy. Something he can chew easy. No nuts. I don't digest nuts. Make yourself at home. Relax. You got some spare time? A little? I got plenty.

When I first started in this business, I rented a place in the center of Miami. Two rooms and a closet. I had a hand-painted sign on the door. Big gold letters: Harry Lipkin. Private Investigator. Standard Rates. It was on the third floor of a block on Camilo Avenue and cost me forty bucks a month.

Now I work from home. My card says 1909 Samuel Gompers Avenue, Warmheart, Florida. There's also a zip code I can never remember. Since no one writes anymore it doesn't bother me. My license I keep in the desk drawer, along with my .38, a box of slugs, my clothes brush, and a spare set of dentures. I might not be the best but I am certainly the oldest.

These days I deal mostly with the sort of cases the cops don't want. Cops want serial homicide. It makes them feel good when they catch someone. But how tough is it to catch a serial killer? You put his picture on TV. Nationwide. You wait. Ten days later a schoolteacher on her lunch break spots him. He's walking out of a Baskin Robbins in a hick town somewhere in Montana. That's him. The guy whose picture was on TV. Before you know it he's surrounded by a million armed cops telling him to drop everything and freeze. And then they shoot him. Ninety-nine cents' worth of vanilla, banana, and pista-chio ice cream wasted.

You want to know about my home? The place I leave for the grocery store. The place I come back to from the grocery store. I'll tell you.

Warmheart is an architectural folly. A mix of Flemish and Florida. It was put up by a homesick Belgian called Herman Van Dood. He built it to look just like the town he left behind when the Germans took over in 1914. The houses are single story but with slate roofs thirty feet high. The incline is sixty-five degrees. Everyone else in Miami has a flat roof. You can stand on it and watch the sun go down. On mine you'd need to be a mountaineer.

Last month a hurricane took half the tiles off. Big

heavy gray slate tiles. Van Dood imported them from Liège. They landed on the grass. They're still there. Some busted into bits. Some are half buried in what used to be the lawn when I cared about lawns. The tiles don't bother me either. But they bother the woman next door. Mrs. Feldman.

"When you gonna get those tiles put back?" she yells. "You think this is Gaza? It looks like a bomb zone."

I tell Mrs. Feldman I don't pay rent to climb ladders.

So. Here I am. No family and no buddies. Issy. Joe. Angelo from Napoli. Big Mal. Little Mal. Manny. Ike. All gone. My oldest buddy died last Purim. Abe Schultz. Born the same year. Same street. Abe's parents were Dutch Jews. Old man Schultz made cigars. They both had mustaches. His was a handlebar with waxed ends. Hers? Well. You couldn't wax the ends. Abe was a dentist before he retired. He made the spare set I keep in the desk drawer. He only charged me for the materials. Abe was that kind of a mensch.

People ask me. Clients. Usually clients. Clients with time on their hands. Were you ever married? I don't mind. They can ask what they like. I charge by the day.

I did try marriage. But it didn't last. I married Nancy. She had long legs and soft lips. Nancy was twenty years old when we got married. Just twenty. Twenty-one when she walked out. I came home one night late from a stake-out and she was gone. No note. Nothing. Just an empty clothes closet and the faint smell of her ten-cent per-fume.

This office has a lot less space than the one I had before. So when I get a client I sit them in the yard. I got a little table and a couple of garden chairs. Plastic with cushions. Yellow. Bright yellow I can see easy. I picked them up in a garage sale. Three bucks and fifty cents. A table and two chairs. For another fifty cents the guy also threw in an umbrella.

Like the suit? I wear it to meet new clients. Brooks Brothers. Seersucker. Classic. 1953. Single-breasted. Loose fit, so the front doesn't go all baggy when I strap on my .38. Perfect for Miami in the summer. It is the same suit that I put on to meet Mrs. Norma Weinberger. Except there was no Mrs. Weinberger.

TWO

Harry Meets His Client

I didn't hear the doorbell ring. But I heard the yard phone extension. It's on the wall by my back door. I had it fixed so I didn't have to leave the tiles and weeds every time someone wanted to talk to me down the wire.

I picked up the handset and said my name.

It was Mrs. Weinberger. She was here. She hadn't forgotten or got lost. She was out front. Calling from her cell phone to say she had rung the bell she didn't know how many times and was I deaf?

I hung up without a reply and went and let her in.

Once I could have made the yard to the front door in under fifteen seconds. These days I am a lot slower. I am a lot slower all round. Pole vaulting. Rock climbing. Doing the mambo. Slow.

I arrived in just under four minutes and opened up.

She was dressed in a pale green polka-dot sleeveless dress and her feet were squeezed into a pair of flat silver slingbacks. Her purse matched the shoes.

The woman looked at me the way they do these days. A private investigator? At your age? A retired rabbi, maybe. But a flatfoot? You got to be kidding.

"Mr. Lipkin?" she said.

I nodded.

The woman put the cell phone in her purse.

"I am Mrs. Weinberger. I have an appointment."

I held out a hand. It waited. It got lonely. I took it back.

"Please come in," I said and led her out to the yard.

We passed framed photos of me in the army. Me out of the army. Me and some buddies. Me on my own. The photos were there to cover the buck-a-roll wallpaper. Big flowers and leaves and damp coming through. When we got to the fresh air I pointed to the chair most in the shade.

"Make yourself at home," I said. "If you need a cushion, I can fetch one from the lounge."

My client replied that she didn't need a cushion and sat down. I sat opposite.

I guessed her age was somewhere in the mid-seventies. When a woman spends a lot of money to stay fifty for the rest of her life it is hard to tell. Dietrich looked better a week before she passed on than some of the kids today do at twenty.

The woman across from me was edgy. The stiff way she was sitting. Like she was wishing she hadn't come.

A lot of clients find it tough to get started. They are embarrassed. Scared. Confused. They put up a front. It's natural. A private dick gets used to it. You go along with it. If you don't you can be there all day talking about everything else but why they are there.

I smiled in a way that said take it easy. Relax. Old Harry will take care of whatever it is. I took a pencil from my jacket pocket. The notebook was on the table. I opened up to a fresh page.

"You want to give me the story so far?" I asked.

She was looking at the lawn.

"Those the tiles?" she said with her eyes fixed on the heap. "Creepy crawlies get to living under tiles. Horrible things. They need tidying up."

"It's on my list," I said. "Now. How can I help?"

She moved her shoulders. Not a shrug. Kind of a loosening up. Mrs. Weinberger had shoulders that were deep tanned. Soft looking. Ample. They were shoulders you grow fond of. She took a breath. Then let go. Some of it came out.

"I am the widow of the late Isaac Weinberger. The most famous hat maker in the whole USA. Weinberger's of New Jersey. The factory was just outside Newark. We lived in an apartment overlooking Central Park. He had a stroke and the doctors advised him to sell up and go somewhere warm. To take it easy. So he did. We have been here ten years. He passed away last July. The twentieth. One minute he was here, the next he was gone. No pain, thank God."

"Thank God."

There was a silence. She looked at the wedding ring on her finger. Then she looked at me.

"We were not blessed with children, Mr. Lipkin."

Some sadness arrived. It hung around. Then it went.

"Can I begin by asking your address," I said. "For my report. I have to provide one. It is statutory."

"Our home is just outside Fort Lauderdale," she said.

I made a note.

"It is very old," she went on. "Spacious and very, very beautiful. We looked at hundreds before we decided on Coral Gables. It took months. Then when we walked up the hill and opened the gates it was love at first sight. Only then, it was called Bella Vista. We had it changed to Coral Gables because Coral Gables is where Mr. Weinberger and I spent our first night together here. I call it my dream home, Mr. Lipkin. So did Mr. Weinberger."

So far I was big on Weinberger history and short on why she had booked a visit. I decided to make it easy for the both of us. I'd ask her. But she beat me to it.

"Mr. Lipkin," she said. "I know what you are thinking. Why am I here?"

I didn't get a chance to reply.

"Someone in my home is stealing from me. Someone I employ. Trust. Care for. Treat like one of the family."

A tear rolled down her cheek. I wrote the word "theft" on my pad and underlined it.

"And what was it?" I asked. "The item that was stolen."

My client found a lace and linen handkerchief in her purse and wiped away the tear. "A pillbox."

I had expected to hear a hundred-carat diamond tiara at the very least. But a pillbox?

"Can you describe it?" I asked.

"What's there to describe?"

"Anything you can think of."

"It's a pillbox. What else? Porcelain with a gold catch and hinges."

"Color?"

"Turquoise."

"Fancy or plain?"

"There's a hand-painted rose on the lid."

"Is the box round or oblong?"

"Heart shaped."

"And the value?"

"Isaac gave it to me. It was for nothing special. Not my birthday, or our wedding anniversary. Just a gift."

"Was the name Limoges printed on the bottom?"

"I think so."

I thought so too and wrote it down.

"Since my pillbox was stolen, Mr. Lipkin," she said, "I haven't had a wink of sleep."

"You think maybe the thief is planning on stealing something else?"

She shook her head. "My sleeping pills are in the box."

I said nothing. A plane flew overhead. One of hundreds that fly over Warmheart. Day and night. South to Miami International.

"When did you notice the box had been stolen?" I said finally.

"Last Friday. They were late delivering the challahs."

"And when was that?"

"About eight-thirty in the evening," she said. "I had just been watching a film on TV. It was with Rock Hudson and Doris Day. When I was younger, people used to tell me I looked just like her. But with dark hair. Doris Day, they would say. She's you. With blond hair. Could be your twin. Personally, I thought I looked more like Lana Turner. But Lana Turner couldn't sing like Doris Day, and I used to do quite a lot of singing. I sang at weddings mostly. They'd ask me, Norma, sing something. Sing Gershwin. Sing 'The Man I Love.' And who was I to say no?"

I left it hanging without an answer for a few seconds.

Then I said, "Do you have any idea how many people might be involved?"

Norma Weinberger shook her head.

"I have a butler. I have a cook. I have a gardener. I have a maid. And I have a chauffeur."

I counted them on my fingers. A handful.

"Have you been to the police?"

Mrs. Weinberger patted her permed hair. At the back. The way a lot of women do when they are put on the spot.

"The police only come when you shoot someone," she said. "And only then if you happen to be a film star or big on TV."

I made a note that the police had not been informed.

"Mr. Lipkin," she went on, "please understand. It isn't the pillbox. It is the idea that I am employing someone who thinks so little of me they would steal from me."

"And it has to be an employee?" I asked. "You are absolutely certain about that?"

She nodded.

"I rarely have guests. Only friends stop by. I live more or less a solitary life."

I wrote it all down but it didn't add up. Who would go to the trouble of stealing a pillbox that cost a couple of hundred bucks at most from a woman worth millions? To find the answer might be worth me taking the case. That and my fifty a day plus expenses. I closed my notebook.

"I will need to talk to all the people who work for you," I told her. "Anytime that suits you is fine."

"I will send the chauffeur to pick you up at three," she said. "Tomorrow afternoon."

Older women usually have problems when they put on lipstick. No matter what color or how much. They usually miss. But not Mrs. Weinberger. She was good. No smudge. No paint on the teeth. When Mrs. Weinberger pulled back her lips the paint went with them. All of it.

Mrs. Weinberger opened her purse.

"A retainer," she said and handed me a crisp hundred-dollar bill. "Isaac believed in them and so do I."

THREE

Harry Meets the Chauffeur

The chauffeur arrived at three on the dot. He drove a salmon pink 1964 Cadillac Eldorado convertible with whitewall tires and parked it tidily in the street. The man was big. Broad across the shoulders. Black skinned. He'd been given a lovat green uniform and a peaked cap. The jacket could have been a size bigger except they probably don't come a size bigger.

He opened the rear passenger door without a word and I climbed in. He said nothing when he closed the door. Mrs. Weinberger's chauffeur had the look of a man who would never say much. Or anything.

We drove north. On one side were tall yellow stucco walls fronting high-rent condominiums and hotels. On the other, sand and the Atlantic Ocean. Lots of sand. But no conversation. Half an hour on the road. Not a word.

I tried forcing it every couple of miles. "Nice car." Nothing. "Nice day." Nothing. "Nice day to have a nice car."

But if the guy at the wheel didn't want to talk to me I had to talk to him. It was the reason for the hundred-dollar bill in my billfold.

I decided to give him one of those questions you have to answer. It wasn't hard. It wasn't, what is the ratio of a square root of the power of a minus ten multiplied by the angle of the circumference? Or, how can anyone eat chicken soup without matzo balls?

It was this. "What's your name, bud? First name, second name, and any you can think of in the middle."

It always works. I say always. Mostly. It worked then.

His reply was soft-spoken. Evenly paced. Not exactly polite but not rude either.

"Rufus. Rufus Davenport. They didn't give me anything in the middle."

"Too bad," I said. "A middle name adds class."

I watched his reflection in the driver's rearview mirror. He used the tip of his index finger to push the peak of his cap an inch up his forehead. The ring on the finger was gold. Thick. Solid. Expensive. I kept it going.

"Have you been driving for Mrs. Weinberger for long?"

"I don't keep a diary."

"A guess costs nothing."

"A year. Maybe more."

"And before?"

His eyes were fixed on the highway. "Before this? I drove trucks. Coast to coast."

He left a silence. Wandered around in it. Then he gave me some answers I didn't ask for.

"When I got drafted they posted me to Alabama. They gave me a tank. 'Drive that, black boy,' they said. And I did. Straight through the commander's office."

He laughed to himself and gently shook his head.

"Two years in an army jail. You learn plenty."

I looked at his hands. They were big. The gold rings would glint from time to time as the sun hit them through the gaps in the palm trees along the highway.

We slowed for lights.

"You a cop?" he said.

I took out my notebook.

"Private."

"I figured it. You don't look like a regular cop."

"I just look old," I said.

He almost laughed.

"You got kids, Mr. Davenport?"

"Three of each." Pride crept in. "My eldest boy is seventeen. You never saw more beautiful girls."

I made a note. Six children. I wondered how much he took home. He was a step ahead of me.

"This job pays well," he said. "Better than most."

He turned and looked at me. Full in the face.

"When I need extra, I fight. In a ring."

It didn't surprise me.

"Win many?" I asked. "It's a tough game."

The chauffeur took one hand off the wheel and turned it into a fist. He held it up. Close to my nose. It was as big as a man's skull.

"The last guy I hit with this is still asleep . . . on a drip."

The lights let us go. There was traffic in front. Rufus Davenport rammed his toe on the gas pedal and we overtook a Nissan pickup full of melons and a German sports car full of a woman talking into a cell phone. Clear of traffic, we dropped back down to the limit along an open stretch of highway.

"Mrs. Weinberger has been the victim of theft," I said as we cruised. "She thinks it might be someone who works for her."

Rufus Davenport said some more nothing. Half a mile. He checked the rearview mirror again and swung the car off the highway onto a narrow road that rose sharply. The car's Hydramatic transmission moved down the gears to take on the incline.

"Mrs. Weinberger only tells me where she wants to go," he said. "Everything else is her business. I don't ask and she doesn't say."

We drove up a narrow road and turned onto a winding slip road that was little more than a path and arrived at a pair of iron gates protecting a one-story mansion that was now clearly visible. The gates were slung between stout redbrick pillars and lions sat on the pillars. Stone lions. Lions with wild eyes and open mouths. Lions like they carved in the old China. Before they gave up carving lions for building washing machines and ten-for-a-dime T-shirts.

Rufus Davenport took a gadget out of the glove compartment and pressed a button. The gates swung open and we rolled forward slowly into the drive.

"I will need to talk to everyone at some time," I said. "Nothing personal, you understand. It's my job."

He nodded. "I'm here six days a week. But only the days."

"Nights?"

He didn't say. The silence said I shouldn't ask.

We pulled up to the door and I got out.

I watched Rufus Davenport back Mrs. Weinberger's spotless antique automobile professionally through the mouth of the Coral Gables garage. I heard the engine cut and a door slam. But I didn't see the chauffeur leave. I guessed there must have been an exit in the far wall. The garage door closed automatically. A single clink of metal against metal in an otherwise silent and empty drive.

I stood there thinking. Harry, I thought. You read *Boxing News*. You read it every week. You have read it since you were a kid. Cover to cover. Every page. The rankings. The title fights. The fights no one much cares about. Yet you never read the name Rufus Davenport. Not once.

· FOUR ·

Harry Arrives at Coral Gables

I went to Mrs. Weinberger's porch and gave the place the once-over. I looked in a flowerpot for discarded evidence. I checked for signs of false entry and examined the earth near the steps for fresh footprints. Standard procedure. Nothing so far. The double door was covered in gloss white paint and plenty of brass that looked like it saw a rag and polish once a day. And it smelled like it. Like the cutlery in the drawer of the cupboard in my bubba's house when she'd been busy with the Brasso. The buzzer was set into the bricks next to a violet creeper.

I thought about buzzers. A dick presses all kinds. Most chime. Ding-dong. That's it. Ding-dong. Sometimes a buzzer plays a simple song. I once had a client who was a TV star. His buzzer played the program's theme. It lasted five minutes. I pressed Mrs. Weinberger's buzzer. Ding-dong.

The butler who opened the door was Asian. Medium height. Medium build. Medium age. Dark hair. Dark eyes. Dark bow tie. I had him down as dark and medium. I introduced myself.

"We have been expecting you, sir," he said with a bow.

He took me through the lobby and showed me into a long and high double room that led onto the poolside.

The butler gestured toward a pale pink velvet sofa big enough to seat the front row of a jury.

"Please take a seat, sir. I shall inform Mrs. Weinberger that you have arrived."

I did as he said.

The pink velvet clashed with my tie. It was the bright yellow one covered with lucky red horseshoes. I eased myself onto a cushion and placed my Panama hat beside me. Then I took a look around.

Jews play the violin. Discover streptomycin. Jews make the best suits and even better corned beef sandwiches. But interior design? What does a Jew do? He pays a fortune to someone with no taste to go to an auction.

The floor was imported white Italian marble. It was covered with a mix of somber Sarouk Persian carpets and bright handwoven Mexican rugs. The mirrors were French. Louis XIV. Gold was everywhere. On candlesticks. On the frames around paintings. On clocks. Half the paintings were the kind you see people walking past in a modern art museum. The other half were by old Dutch masters. Windmills. Skaters. Taverns full of guys smoking pipes, drinking beer, and playing cards. The art collection was hung between the mirrors. One wall was covered by an eighteenth-century Flemish tapestry. Under it was a neoclassical Italian marquetry commode. It was the kind of thing Lucretia Borgia kept her poisons in. These days you don't need poison to kill someone. You just feed them fast food for a month. More or less in the middle of the room was a white Steinway and a stool. Top-end Steinway. The sort Liberace smiled on beside the candelabra. The shut lid was a home for photos of the Weinberger family. A lot of them were of Mrs. Weinberger when she looked like Doris Day. But with dark hair. They were arranged around a tall vase filled with a dozen fresh-cut lilac gladioli.

Added together the contents of the room were worth a couple of million bucks. And yet someone stole a pill-box worth a couple of hundred.

There was the sound of heels on marble.

Mrs. Weinberger came and stood in front of me. She was wearing a full-length pale blue cotton bathrobe. On her head was a pale green towel wrapped into a turban. Her peep-toe bedroom slippers were pale pink satin with pale pink pompoms. Pale shades and Mrs. Weinberger.

The two went together. You didn't need to be a detective to discover it.

"I hope you haven't been too bored waiting, Mr. Lipkin," she said in a way that didn't require an answer.

There was a matching easy chair facing the sofa. Mrs. Weinberger sat and draped one leg over the other. Her robe slipped open a little. At her ankles. A painted toe peeped up at me.

"I have arranged for you to talk to Maria to begin with," she said. "Maria Lopez is my maid."

She took out a sheet of writing paper folded in two from a pocket in her robe and handed it over.

"What you have there, Mr. Lipkin, is a list of the names of the five people who work for me. Including Maria. You can choose a time for yourself when it is most suitable to talk with the others. I will make it clear why you are here and that they are to cooperate fully. I want this whole dreadful business cleared up. And I want it done soon."

I gave the list a glance and placed it under my hat.

"I'll do what I can, and as soon as is possible," I said.

Mrs. Weinberger sighed. It sounded like a sigh of contentment. But then some people have a laugh that sounds like an attack of asthma. You can never be sure. She picked up the bone china bell from the occasional table beside her and made it tinkle.

"Will Maria be with you long, Mr. Lipkin?" my client asked when the tinkling stopped.

"It depends," I said. "Some people tell lies more convincingly than others. Is there some kind of hurry?"

Mrs. Weinberger nodded at the pool. "Not exactly. It is just that I swim at this time of day. Maria always helps me dry off."

She put the bell down.

"Half an hour should be plenty," I told her.

Mrs. Weinberger stood up. "Maria is on her way. Can I get her to bring you a drink? Lemon tea, perhaps?"

"A glass of water would be just fine," I said. "I have to take my pill. Four-thirty. Every day. Heartburn."

Maria's employer gave me a sweet, wholesome, sympathetic smile. The sort Doris Day invented.

"I take mine before I go to bed," she said.

FIVE

Harry Meets the Maid

Maria brought me a cut-glass tumbler of water with ice on a silver tray and put it on the coffee table. I took my pill and thanked her.

Mrs. Weinberger's maid was just over five foot in a crisp white top, a fresh starched apron, a short dark skirt, dark stockings, and flat shoes.

"Take a seat, Miss Lopez," I said.

She sat across from me with her knees close together and her hands clasped tightly on her lap.

"I am a private detective," I explained. "My name is Harry Lipkin. I am going to ask you a few simple questions. Just routine. There is no need to worry. It is what detectives do."

"I know," Maria Lopez said.

Her voice was soft with plenty of Spanish accent still on show.

"I watch detectives on TV. Columbo," she went on. "He is my favorite. You know. He says, 'Just one more thing.' Goes out and comes back. 'Just one more thing.' He makes me laugh."

I smiled and took out my notebook and pencil.

"Watch a lot of TV?" I asked. "This job must keep you pretty busy."

She got herself into a more relaxed pose.

"You are right, Señor," she said. "Here I am on duty all the time. But I watch TV a lot back home. It is how to learn talking English. With the TV."

"And where is home?" I asked.

"La Paz." She said the name the way people talk about a sacred shrine. "It is in Bolivia."

I smiled. "Was the last time I looked."

"You have been there?" she asked. I shook my head. "It is beautiful, Señor Lipkin. The mountains. Cold at the top. Ice and snow. On the land. On the earth and the fields. Hot like here. But better. The earth is rich. Everything grows good. Rich. Everything." She could see it all.

I left her looking for a moment. Then I asked.

"Maria, how long have you worked for Mrs. Weinberger?"

"Not for so long," she said and relaxed some more. "My sister, Paquita, she was the maid to Mrs. Weinberger before me."

I made a note.

"And what happened to Paquita?"

"Nothing bad for Paquita," Maria said. "It is because of my father."

I raised what had once been an eyebrow.

"Your father?"

"He is sick. Paquita, Señor, she has gone back to look after him."

"Sorry to hear it," I said. "Is the sickness serious? Not that you need to tell me."

Maria fiddled with the edge of her skirt.

"I don't mind to tell, Señor," she said. "He worked in a coal mine. One day the mine, it collapsed. My father was there ten days. No food. No water. Many died."

"But your father got out? And he got sick from being trapped? That it?"

She nodded. "Sí, Señor. His lungs. His breathing. They are not good. He walks for a few minutes. He stands. And then he is fighting for life. Coughing. Holding his chest in pain."

She pulled the hem of her skirt to try to cover more of her knees. It's the kind of little distraction people do when they are anxious. It's the kind of thing detectives make a mental note of. And if I hadn't been working I would have enjoyed the shape a lot more. They were pretty knees. Firm. Not too much flesh. Not too little.

Perfect. Señorita Lopez was perfect all over but for a tiredness just about visible around her wide and deep-as-a-lake eyes.

"When was that?" I asked. "The coal mine."

"Señor?"

"When did it collapse?"

She thought about it.

"I don't exactly remember. We were all so shocked and scared for my father. Two years. Maybe more."

I wrote down some of it.

"Can you be specific?" I asked.

The maid hesitated.

"Is it important?"

"I don't know," I said. "The fact is miners who get killed when shafts collapse make the news. No matter where. Pittsburgh. Peking. La Paz. The more men who die, the bigger the story. I never saw or heard anything about a coal mine disaster in La Paz. How come?"

Maria gave it some more thought before replying. I knew she would.

"More men were injured than were killed. Just a few. Maybe that is why you never heard the story."

"That must be it," I said.

It was my turn to leave a little silence. Then I asked her.

"Couldn't your mother look after your father?"

Maria made the sign of the cross. Just once. Across her heart.

"My mother. She is dead. It happened when I was still only a little girl. Then my Aunt Rosa helped my father. But she is now also dead."

It sounded like a lot of dead close relatives for one so young and beautiful. But I didn't say so. Instead I stood up and walked to the window. I could see Mrs. Weinberger in the pool doing her version of swimming. She was belly down on a floating recliner paddling with her hands. There was a straw beach hat covering her head. A backless one-piece and plenty of sunblock covered the rest. Only a steamship out of coal moved slower. I went and sat down again. I had work to do.

"Doctors and drugs cost money," I said.

"A lot of money."

"And the mining company? Do they give you help?"

Maria Lopez shook her head angrily. "They give us nothing but excuses. Nothing."

"So who pays the bills? You?"

Her eyes looked into her lap.

"I save," she said. "And I send something home each month. It is all my father has to keep him alive. Paquita cannot work because my father needs her with him all the time."

I felt bad having to put her through my questions but that was the deal. It was my job. I spoke as kindly as I knew.

"Is there no one else in your family, apart from you,

your sister, and your father?" I asked her. "Brothers maybe? To lend a hand?"

Maria nodded.

"Manuel and Diego. They are older. So is Paquita. I am the youngest of the family. I will be nineteen in June."

"Your brothers. Are they here, in Miami?"

"Both. Diego has a job. He works in a casino. In Sunny Isles Beach. The Four Aces."

"And can't he help with the medicine and doctors?"

"He is getting married next year. Weddings also cost money. And to buy a house. You must know, Señor. In the United States, everything," her voice trailed off, "it all costs so much . . ."

I wrote down *Brother getting married so can't help pay for sick Pappy* and underlined it.

"And Manuel?" I asked. "What's stopping Manuel dropping into Western Union from time to time? Not planning to marry as well, is he?"

There was a very long pause. I could have read a whole sentence by Proust. She didn't want to answer. There was trouble in the air. You knew it. The brother was *tsuris*, trouble. I tried again. I did it gentle.

"If there is something you'd rather not tell me," I said, "I can't make you. I am only a private cop, trying to find out who is stealing from Mrs. Weinberger. I promise, not a word will go further than this room."

It did the trick. She let it out.

"Manuel. He is a good boy, Mr. Lipkin. He means well. But he is always in trouble. He is not like Diego. Quick to learn. Manuel only learns from bad men. The gangs. The men he hangs out with."

It was a big admission. It kind of took the life out of her. She was a small size to start with. Now she seemed to be hardly there.

I stood up again and could see Mrs. Weinberger climbing out of the pool. It was time to let Maria off the hook and let her get on with toweling water off Mrs. Weinberger's body.

"Thanks, Maria," I said. "That will be all for the time being."

A couple of tears slid down Maria's cheeks. She wiped them away with the end of her apron and took a deep breath. "Thank you, Señor. For your understanding."

She stood and without another word ran to the pool. Only a young gazelle ran more gracefully.

Harry Meets the Butler

watched as Maria helped Norma Weinberger climb from the steps at the shallow end of the pool. She climbed easily for a woman her age. A lot more elegantly than she swam. Even without Maria I guess she would have made it to dry land in style. I moved through the French doors to get a better view of my client.

She had put on a pair of buttercup yellow sunglasses with rims the size of truck wheels and was in a backless lime green number with a double fronted bodice and side ruching in a material they called Lastex. Jantzen labeled the swimsuit Water Star and it would have cost sixty dollars when it went on sale in 1954. Sixty dollars, ninety-five cents to be exact. I know about swimsuits. I had an uncle who sold them. Uncle Enoch. He talked a lot about them. To me. To everyone. Uncle Enoch talked about nothing else.

The pool led onto the lawn and there were clusters of high-crowned long-ago-planted palms everywhere. The palms dwarfed the row of low buildings that rimmed the horizon. These were a different style from the house. Newer. The place where Mrs. Weinberger lived was mainly a single story that snaked its way around the flower beds. To the right were stables but no sign of any horses. Maybe they were sleeping. It was a good time to be asleep. Hot. Exhaustingly hot. Even for Miami.

I walked back to air-conditioned comfort and sat on the piano stool. I looked at my notebook and thought about what I had written.

So far I had spoken to the chauffeur and the maid. That left the gardener and the cook and the butler. Any friends that called I could forget. My guess was they were all as wealthy. Some more. And I didn't see some old Jew risking a busted neck climbing over the wall in the middle of the night just to steal a pillbox. What would be her motive?

When someone commits the crime of theft the motive is nearly always money. And for a professional there is no other. He steals a famous painting. A Rembrandt. From a gallery in Idaho where someone left the back door unlocked. He takes it to a fence who pays him cash. On a Rembrandt the fence sells for ten million the thief will pocket ten grand. Only hungry people steal food and only people who need mental help steal from compulsion.

Maria Lopez might need extra money to help her father back in La Paz. So might Rufus Davenport. I'd make some inquiries about both. Ask around boxing gyms. The Immigration Department. City Hall. I finished reading through my notes to the sound of a polite cough. The butler was standing discreetly behind me.

"I am Lee," the butler announced. "We met briefly, earlier, you may recall, when you arrived."

"Hello," I said. "Nice to meet you again."

"Mrs. Weinberger said you wished to see me."

"Only a few routine questions," I said. "Okay with you?"

His head moved. I guessed it meant yes.

"That's my man," I said. "Grab a seat. Ease the dogs."

He remained motionless. He was in a white jacket that had never seen a crease and black pants that knew a white jacket to live under when one came along.

"If it is all the same to you, sir," he said, "I feel more at ease when standing."

"Fine by me," I said. "But if I stand for more than ten minutes I get pains in my legs and my blood pressure goes up. I have even been known to pass out if I am on my feet too long. Avoid a long line. That's my motto."

I had hoped a little personal confession might warm

the butler up. Maybe get a smile. I was wrong. His face had features. Eyes. A nose. A mouth. But they showed less expression than a plate of pickled smelts. And they stayed that way.

"Do you live here, in the house?" I asked.

He was standing with his back to the window. A cloud moved slowly across the clear blue sky behind his head. In the distance was the thin buzz of someone driving an electric mower over grass.

"All the staff live here," he said. "We have our own quarters."

The butler made a half turn and gestured to the low buildings at the far end of the lawn. "Mrs. Weinberger has grown less independent in recent years. Lately, she has asked me to retire in the main house. To be near if I am required."

"So you have pretty much the run of the place?" I said. "Come and go as you please. Just like you were one of the family?"

Mr. Lee's slender eyes did something. At the back. And only for a split second. Something dark.

"I am Mrs. Weinberger's butler," he said. "It is my duty, as well as my desire, to aid Mrs. Weinberger whenever I am needed. No matter what hour of the day."

"Devotion," I said. "Rare to find these days. Worth paying a lot for."

The butler said nothing.

Sitting in front of the piano keys I thought I might try a few bars of "Chopsticks." To sort of lighten up the mood. Then I thought. Harry. "Chopsticks" after eighty years? Without practice?

Instead I asked the butler another question.

"When Mrs. Weinberger discovered someone had been stealing from her, did she tell you?"

"Naturally," Mr. Lee replied. "Last week she said a pill-box had gone missing. Then she said some house keys and a cheap fan were taken."

"And you saw no one suspicious around the house at the times these items were taken?"

The butler shook his head. More of a twitch than a shake.

"I was only informed of the missing item later."

"So you could have been quite near to the thief, or right at the other end of the house? You could have been just about anyplace?"

His eyes didn't like me. Or my questions. Or the implied accusation.

"That is most possible, sir," he said. "But also most unlikely. I seldom fail to observe any actions that take place in the house that might be considered irregular."

I looked at my watch. I had still to see the cook and the gardener once he got through with his mowing.

"Thank you, Mr. Lee," I said.

He bowed. "Will that be all, sir?" he asked.

"From you," I said. "For the moment. Now I have to talk to the man in charge of rolling knaidlach."

"You are referring to the chef, I assume?"

"The very man," I smiled. "Will you kindly point me in the direction of the cookhouse?"

"Follow me, sir," the butler said.

We were about to move off when some thoughts started connecting in my head. It was like in the old days when they turned on the lights in Times Square. The lights came on in a line. One after the other. Fast. That is what was happening in Harry's cranium. They connected like this. "Chopsticks." The sound of Mahjong tiles. A stack of blue chips. A winning post. Some thoughts connecting up and a good old-fashioned hunch to hold them together. Every detective needs one. A hunch. Like he needs his .38. His license and his gumshoes.

I called to the butler by his name.

"Mr. Lee."

"Sir?"

"Horse racing," I chimed. "The track. A very popular sport. Here. Everywhere. Compulsive for some. You couldn't keep my Uncle Benny away. Gulfstream is under an hour's drive. A dollar buys a hundred when the information's right. Hard to resist. A place you might go?"

The butler stiffened. A response given away outside his usual tight control. And he knew it. And he knew I knew. And he didn't like it.

Mr. Lee looked at his fingernails to cover. As if they suddenly bothered him. They were trimmed close to the skin and buffed hard. Clean as hubcaps on a showroom automobile.

Then the stiffness went and he looked me straight in the eye.

"Mrs. Weinberger's chef is a busy man, sir," Mrs. Weinberger's man said. "We must not keep him waiting any longer."

SEVEN

Harry and Mr. Lee Walk to the Kitchen

The cookhouse was a schlep and a half. The butler walked ahead of me. Slow. In keeping with my pace.

"The kitchen was refurbished last fall," Mr. Lee explained as we shuffled over the fancy tiled floor. "It is fully equipped with all the latest in culinary conveniences."

"So there is a lot to keep the chef occupied?" I said.

He nodded.

"And there's the Kosher food side of it all to take care of," I carried on. "I guess the cook fixes that?"

The butler turned and waited for me to draw level.

"There is a high-class Kosher delicatessen in Fort Lauderdale," he said. "They deliver once a week, so the chef has no need to shop. My duties as Mrs. Weinberger's manservant include the supervision and purchase of all edible goods brought into the house. I also ensure they are in exact accordance with Mrs. Weinberger's strict religious observances. In the unlikely event something should go wrong, it is my duty to put it right."

None of the information mattered. It was either handed out to kill time or throw me off the scent, except that there wasn't any scent. Not yet.

"That is all very interesting," I said in a way to show it wasn't.

There was a short silence while I made a few more feet.

"Mr. Lee?" I said when I drew level. "I hope it doesn't bother you but I got to ask. It has been on my mind right from the get-go. How come you talk English so good?"

The butler left it a second. Like he was about to give an estimate for replacing the air-conditioning. Then he told me. Matter of fact. Without a hint of sounding smug.

"I learned English in England," he said. "I was educated in a town called Newbury. It is regarded as one of the world's centers for breeding Thoroughbred racehorses. The stud farms of Newbury are second to none. There, I met men who were highly knowledgeable. Professional men. As you have already quite impressively deduced for yourself, I practice the skills they taught me at the Gulfstream Park Racing & Casino racetrack. And I do so, if you will forgive the slight immodesty offering such information entails, most successfully."

There was another short silence. It was there for me to file his story. Then we walked on.

And on.

And on.

"How long is this passage?" I asked. "We must be in Tallahassee."

"Not much further, sir," the butler replied soothingly. "And it might be worth noting, sir, that Tallahassee is north from here. We are walking in the opposite direction."

The south-bound passage hit a fork. We took the left lane.

"The kitchen has a view overlooking the Atlantic," the butler continued. "As I am sure you have already observed, this house is very close to the sea. The beach is just below the cliff on which the foundations were originally laid, more than a hundred years ago."

"No kidding," I slipped in. "That long ago?"

"You can feel the breeze most days," he continued as if I hadn't spoken. "A breeze that brings with it a sense of distant lands and their distant peoples. The far off which is ever present."

"You sure have a swell turn of phrase, Mr. Lee," I said. "Imaginative and philosophic. I'll try to incorporate that last thought of yours into a haiku when I get a spare moment."

He left it. Then brought it back.

"It is the Japanese who compose haiku. The Chinese occupy their minds in more useful ways."

Suddenly, Mrs. Weinberger appeared from a sliding door that led onto another passage that led onto a room next to the lounge.

She'd got Maria to help her into a pair of pale linen slacks and a plain silk top with faux jet buttons. In one hand she was holding a tall glass of seltzer swamped with fruit salad and a straw. In the other she clutched a paperback.

"You may leave us," Mrs. Weinberger told her butler. "I shall take care of our guest from here."

Mr. Lee marched off. When he was out of sight she held up the book for me to see.

"I have been reading all about you, Mr. Lipkin," Mrs. Weinberger said and sucked on the straw.

I looked at the cover. *The Killer Wore Black.* The title in embossed silver took up half the page. The rest of it was split between the author's name and a picture of a blonde in a low-cut blouse screaming. It was one of a hundred Edward J. Macey had reeled off over the years. *The Killer Wore Black. The Killer Wore Plaid. The Killer Wore Silk. The Killer Smoked Cigars. The Killer Ate Pretzels.*

"Me?" I asked, going along with her train of thought.

"Not you exactly, Mr. Lipkin," she laughed. "No. Your methods. The way a private investigator operates. For example, in chapter ten, when Elliot Sterne discovers the corpse of Charles Billington in the garage, he only tells his brother, so that when his twin sister arrives to identify him, it is clear they never met in Denver after all. Her alibi was already under suspicion."

"That's the way to do it," I said.

She sucked some more seltzer.

"I can't wait to hear what you have found out so far," she said.

There wasn't a lot to tell her. It was too early. Most clients only know detective work from what they see on TV. Or read in pulp fiction. Over in half an hour or a couple of hundred pages. Real life? It can take months to check a single clue. I told Mrs. Weinberger what I told all anxious clients.

"I am getting warm," I said. "The noose is tightening and I am hot on the trail."

"Any minute, then, Mr. Lipkin. And we will nail the culprit."

"Any minute, Mrs. Weinberger."

She gave a deep sigh and pointed. "The kitchen is to the left."

· EIGHT ·

Harry Meets the Chef

When Mr. Lee told me about Coral Gables's kitchen he called it fully equipped. He might be spinning a line about his skills as a punter but he was bang on the nail about the room where Mrs. Weinberger had her meals dished up.

There were machines for slicing carrots, shredding cabbage, extracting juice, pressing oranges, dicing gherkins, crushing ice, kneading bread, boiling rice, frying potatoes, halving avocados, pitting olives, mixing mayonnaise, shelling peas, and whisking eggs. If there was a cement mixer, it wasn't on show.

The cook was over by the sink running water over his hands. He was tall and slender. There was a chef's hat on his head and a red spotted scarf tied loosely under his chin. His skin had the sheen of polished ebony.

"My name is Harry Lipkin," I called over.

The cook wiped his hands dry on the apron covering the front of his blue checkered pants.

"Amos," he called back. "Amos Moses."

I found a stool next to a worktable and perched.

"I understand Mrs. Weinberger told you I would drop by?" I said. "I need to ask a few routine questions. About some thefts that have taken place here in recent weeks."

Amos Moses picked up a tray of cream cheese blintzes and put them in the oven.

"Dinner's due," he said, turning up the heat. "Can we talk while I fix it?"

I nodded.

"Tell me about what you did before you got a job baking blintzes for Mrs. Weinberger," I said.

"Anything in particular?"

"Whatever comes to mind."

"There's not a lot to tell. I left my country when I was sixteen. Ethiopia. Somalia one side. Sudan the other. And Kenya's not far away. Lions here. Malaria over there."

"Did you come to the States direct?"

There was a yolk in a large bowl half full of flour. He started beating it with a whisk.

"I went to Italy first. Then I spent a year in Paris."

He poured milk into the mixture. "Paris is where you learn to cook the world's great dishes. Caille en Sarcophage with truffle sauce. Cream cheese blintzes."

The young cook had a nice style. Direct, but not rude.

And funny in the ways Jews are funny. Self-deprecating on one hand. Arrogant on the other. If Amos Moses hadn't told me I would have said he came from the Lower East Side. I could hear his bubba telling him, "Amos. Listen to your grandmother. Jews own restaurants. They don't cook in them."

"And after Paris, Amos?" I said taking out my notebook and pencil. "What then?"

He put the mixture in the icebox and came and stood across from me.

"I worked my way over on a boat. I found this job through an agency."

I wrote it down. "When was that? Roughly."

"That would be about two years ago. Mr. Weinberger was still alive. He had a big appetite. Even though he was old and pretty sick he ate more chopped liver than anyone I ever met."

I put down when Amos started working for Mrs. Weinberger. I didn't bother with Mr. Weinberger's eating habits. The kitchen was warm. More than warm. It was very hot. Even with the windows open. It must have showed.

"You look like you could use a drink, Mr. Lipkin," Amos said. "I could do fresh pineapple?"

"A drink would be just dandy. But not pineapple. They have acid and I got reflux. Acid and reflux. Bad medicine."

I rubbed my chest to make the point.

"Then I'll do you peach juice," the cook said and picked out a peach from a dish full of fruit. "No acid in peaches."

Amos worked fast with the knife and the fruit. Halved it. Pitted it. Peeled it. He did a handful the same way. Put the flesh into the extractor. Poured in some fresh cream. Spun it. Poured the juice into a frosted glass. Threw in some ice. Stuck in a couple of straws. And there it was. All done in under a minute. Peach juice. Fresh. I took a sip. It was cold. Sweet. Smooth. I put down the glass and picked up my pencil.

"It must get pretty dull at times," I said. "Not a lot to do in a place like this when you aren't cooking blintzes and making old detectives peach juice."

"I got plenty to fill my time," Amos said. "I am helping to build a new synagogue."

The surprise on my face registered. Plain as the mustache Dali painted on the Mona Lisa. But I should have guessed. The name. Amos Moses. Obvious. An Ethiopian Jew. The lost tribe of Israel.

"Some time filler," I said. "Tougher than collecting early Elvis records."

Amos Moses smiled. "A lot tougher."

Then he looked at me. His expression said that there was something I should know. Something he guessed I didn't. He was right.

"There was a war," he said softly. "We lived in a place

called Beta Israel. It was where the war took place. Geno-
cide. Women were raped. Children were murdered.
It seemed like it would never end, but it did. Finally.
Through famine. Through armed rebellion. Then came
the airlift. Operation Solomon. Around twenty thousand
people were airlifted from Ethiopia to Israel. It was the
biggest and most successful airlift the world has ever
known. Imagine it, Mr. Lipkin."

I tried. I failed.

"Thirty-four planes flew nonstop for thirty-six hours,"
Amos carried on. "Almost the entire population of Ethiopian Jews was transported to Israel. But some remained.
Mainly the Falash Mura. These people, under threat of
death by nineteenth-century missionaries, converted to
Christianity. In time they returned to Judaism. The Falash
Mura, who now number around two hundred thousand,
have had the almost impossible task of rebuilding their
lives. Their homes. Their places of worship."

It was some lesson. I knew from Moses and the Red
Sea. Noah. Job. Old history. From Falash Mura? *Nada.*

"Plenty of wealthy Jews around," I said. "You picked
the right spot. Miami's bursting with them."

Amos went and opened the drawer of a small wooden
table in the corner of the kitchen. The kind cooks sit at
to write out recipes. He took out a bundle of letters held
together with a rubber band and placed them in front
of me.

"This is my list," he said. "Alphabetical. I am up to *G*."

I skimmed through half a dozen replies. Amos had written in the amount donated at the top of each letter.

"Impressive," I said. "Guggenheim in particular."

"One or two have been very generous."

I handed Amos the letters. He put them back in the drawer and then turned off the oven.

"Sorry, Mr. Lipkin," he said. "I got to get on with serving supper. But I will keep my ears and eyes open."

"Thanks," I said and put away my notebook. "Nice meeting you, Amos."

He came and stood close. "You, too, Mr. Lipkin."

I climbed off the stool and we shook hands. I looked into his eyes. They were filled with a long journey. Longer than any journey ever made.

· N I N E ·

Harry Meets the Gardener

If old Harry Lipkin took a while getting to the kitchen it took no time at all to locate the gardener. It's simple. Chauffeurs are in automobiles. Chefs are in kitchens. Maids are in parlors. Butlers are there when you call them and gardeners are in gardens.

He was on his knees behind a fancy shrub fixing something on the mower. It was a mower you drive. He was mid-sixties. No extra weight to mention and still big in the places it matters. The upper body. Biceps. Thighs. Neck. He was in a worn T-shirt with the arms torn off. His graying hair was held in a ponytail and there were bead bracelets on both his wrists. He had a gold earring running through his right earlobe and a diamond stuck into his left nostril. Every finger had a ring. The only skin showing was covered with tattoos. Skulls. Daggers. Hearts. Dragons. Mermaids. Swastikas. A lot were worn out. Old. Faded. Indistinct. Others looked more recent. Some quite new. On his left forearm there was one that clearly read *Kill Mankind to Live.*

"My name's Harry," I said over a hedge of thick foliage.

The gardener stopped working and looked up at me. He wanted more. I walked round the evergreen fence and stood close to him.

"Private detective. Mrs. Weinberger hired me. I won't take up a lot of your time."

He stood up. Slow. Very slow. Like standing up was the hardest thing he ever had to do.

"Steve."

"Anything else? For the record."

Steve wiped his hands down his denim pants.

"For the record," he drawled, "if I got called something else, I don't remember it."

I thought about suggesting tincture of ginkgo biloba. It is nature's way of curing memory loss. I read about it once. In the *Reader's Digest.* Or maybe it was *Sports Illustrated.* Either way, I let it go. Steve had the look of a man who remembered and forgot to order.

I rested up against the wheel hub of the mower.

"I need to ask you a few questions, Steve," I said.

"About?"

"General questions. About who might be stealing goods from Mrs. Weinberger."

"And you figure I will have an answer?"

"That's the way it works," I said. "I ask a question. You give me an answer."

Steve took a tan leather tobacco pouch from the rear pocket of his jeans and a packet of King Size Rizlas from another pocket and began rolling himself a smoke.

"An answer is not knowledge," he said. "Truth is never the answer. Truth is only the question. Knowledge is found. Never in an answer."

It was the old Beat jive, Zen, and hippy jargon all molded into one. It convinces some. A fake swami's trick. A dollar a hit. The meaning of life. Snake oil. I took out my notebook and pencil to introduce a sense of formality. A cop's trick.

"You been in the job long?" I asked.

He ran the tip of his tongue expertly over the paper's gummed edge and sealed the weed.

"Last year I was working in Los Angeles," he said. "The year before in New Mexico. Anyplace they got a garden."

The gardener tucked the stick into the corner of his mouth. Then he pulled out a silver Zippo from his vest pocket and lit the cigarette. The smell was a mix of sweet body sweat and burnt molasses and dead leaves.

I tried again to get an answer.

"The question wasn't where, mister. It wasn't what. It was how long? In this job?"

Steve sat cross-legged on the tiled path.

"Time, man," he said. "Everyone is so hung up on time."

"You got something against it?" I asked.

"You can't have something against something that don't exist," he said.

Mrs. Weinberger's gardener uncrossed his legs and stretched out on his back, staring at the sky. He blew smoke from his lips in a thin stream and watched it curl upward.

I left it for a minute or two and I tried another way. "When did you take your first salary check?" I asked.

Steve grinned. Or maybe it was a sneer. One way or another, his mouth did something.

"Salary?"

"The money you have left when they take away the tax."

He sucked in smoke.

"Check me over, friend. My pockets are empty. Lined only with the gold of freedom. Freedom from slavery to the dollar."

It wasn't the answer I had expected. Nor understood or wanted. I moved off from the mower and stood over him.

"Let me get this straight," I said. "Are you telling me you work for free?"

He looked at his slow-burning cigarette and knocked

ash off the butt with a flick of his little finger. The one with a ring shaped into a silver skull with topaz eyes.

"No cents. No dollars. No dimes," he crooned. "I ask only for somewhere to place my head at night and refreshment to sustain the flesh we call our body. What those who have attained enlightenment call the spirit's temporal home."

His gaze drifted toward the garden shed. It was the size of a bungalow. I could see through the open doors all the stuff you need to kill weeds and cut back the ivy. And there was a single bed. Made up. Ready for someone to sleep in.

I jerked a thumb at Steve's temporal home.

"And that's part of the deal?"

He closed his eyes. "A place of spiritual wonder and holiness."

There was a long pause. Then Steve opened his eyes and they searched. Like the beam of a lighthouse searches. Far out. Dreamily. Then they stopped searching and found me.

"Peace of mind, friend," Steve said. "No one owes Steve. And Steve owes no one."

More phony Zen. The philosophy of dope. I looked hard at his forearm. Looking for pinpricks. The tiny holes a needle leaves when you inject your veins with heroin. They would be there. For certain. But I couldn't see them. No one could. Even a young man with a young man's eyes. The inky grime of a tattoo that read *Kill Mankind to Live* was in the way.

I walked back to the Cadillac, where Rufus was waiting. I climbed in and he drove me home.

TEN

Harry Gets a New Message

After talking to everyone I still had nothing worth a page of a report. Not even a paragraph. Each suspect had a motive. Each suspect had access. That was it. My report. Motive and access. It was time I started asking around town to give Mrs. Weinberger something hard to bite on and myself something positive to chase. I needed leads. Contacts. I needed to make a list. Who and what?

I'd start with Rufus. Check with the gyms. Tommy Field's would be a good place to start. But more than anything else I needed to get some sleep. Suddenly I was all in. It was time to give Harry Lipkin's astral body an early promenade among the stars.

I went to bed well before nine. But I didn't sleep. The old never sleep much. It doesn't bother us. We know we'll soon be getting plenty. I got cramps in my left calf and a lot of what I'd eaten kept coming back up the pipe that took it down. Pickled onions and chopped chicken liver. Sure. I have pills. The packet says take two at night. Before you go to bed. It doesn't say what to do if you forget. I slept an hour.

I ate breakfast slowly and didn't hurry doing anything else. Around noon I perked up a little and called Tommy Field's Gym. I said I would drop by in an hour. I was halfway to the front door when the phone rang. I'd programmed the answering machine to let the phone ring seven times before picking up. From the first ring to the last takes twenty-one seconds. I would never make it. Five yards of hallway and another three to the desk. I stood where I was and listened to the voice leaving a message. You can do that with my machine. With the volume up. It was my client.

"Mr. Lipkin. Are you there? It is me. Mrs. Weinberger. Please call me as soon as you can. The thief has struck again. My jade bracelet. I left it on my dressing table last night. This morning it was gone."

The machine clicked and went dead.

There was nothing I could do. A call back would have only wasted my time. Later with the call back. I crossed the front yard to the garage and massaged my Chevy Impala into life.

I aimed it east across the city.

A forty-year-old Chevy Impala isn't a car I would buy. I got given it. I was hired by an Italian called Leo Cardosi.

He owned a restaurant on Dania Beach. Casa Cardosi. He ran it with his younger brother Dino. Leo believed Dino was messing around with his wife. One night they got into a fight and Dino pulled a gun. Dino shot Leo dead and the judge gave him life. A week later the restaurant went out of business. Leo's wife gave me his Chevy as payment. It was all she had.

ELEVEN

Harry Meets Eddie Berkowitz at His Gym

The drive from my little shack in Warmheart to Tommy Field's gym takes half an hour. Finding a place to park takes a hundred years. I found a spot five blocks away. I put change into the meter and walked the half a mile back along NW Eleventh Street to the gym.

If you didn't know Tommy Field had a place to train boxers you'd pass right on by. Tommy's was spread out above a row of stores. You got to it through a narrow door and up a steep flight of steps. There was no sign outside.

Tommy was long gone. He passed on the year they elected Ike. His son Tommy Junior ran it for a while. Then the son sold it to Mike Gutti who sold it to the man I wanted to talk to. He was a trainer called Eddie Berkowitz. I'd known him twenty years. Eddie was an ex-pro. His record was 67 wins, 23 losses, 2 draws. Eddie

Berkowitz knew how to use a left hook. All but seven of his wins were knockouts.

I waited to get my breath back from the walk and then climbed the stairs. A pair of swinging doors took me into a light and airy room. A full-size ring filled most of it. Inside the ropes a couple of kids were busy learning their trade. One was light skinned. The other black. Both had fast feet. Fast hands. Jab. Duck. Jab. Duck. The canvas deck squeaked with every move.

I made my way across the room, passing a flyweight punching a bag twice his size. "Cuba" was written large on his vest. Next to him was an ex-champ in a bright red track suit and brilliant white trainers. The title he won was thirty years ago. When he had hair and a name people knew. He was shouting at the Cuban kid to speed up the combos and keep them coming. Other boxers were just hanging around. Sitting. Sweating. Skipping. All of them were dreaming.

The man I wanted to talk to had his office at the back. Next to the changing rooms and showers. I padded along a wall decorated with posters of great fights. Some Tommy Field had promoted. I read the names. Rocky Marciano. Willie Pepp. Joe Louis. Jack Dempsey. Sugar Ray Robinson. Floyd Patterson. Ezzard Charles. Archie Moore. Roberto Duran. Muhammad Ali. Benny Leonard. If you sang them, they'd sound sweeter than the Song of Solomon.

I knocked on the office door.

"Come in and make yourself at home," a voice called.

I did as I was told.

Eddie Berkowitz was sitting at his desk. He was medium height and had never put on more than a couple of pounds since he quit the ring. He wore his silver hair in an inch-high crew cut and showed plenty of tan on his big arms. In all the years I had known him Eddie Berkowitz had never changed his style of dressing. He wore a cotton pique polo shirt tucked into casual pants. He kept it simple. Like the way he lived his life. Like the way he once boxed.

"Good to see you, Harry," Eddie Berkowitz said and pointed to a vacant seat. "What's on your mind?"

"Rufus Davenport," I said. "The name mean anything?"

He gave it some thought. Then he shook his head.

"Tell me more, Harry."

"He drives the widow of a onetime New York hat maker called Weinberger," I said. "Someone is stealing from her. Most of the stuff is small-time. Trinkets. House keys. Even a cheap fan. But the last I heard they have taken some jade."

Eddie gave a low whistle. "That's serious money."

"A thousand bucks an ounce. More once it's been carved."

"And you figure Rufus Davenport for a suspect?"

BARRY FANTONI

"That's why I am here," I said. "He told me he fights professionally. To make the extra. If I can put a tick against Davenport's story I could maybe eliminate him."

Eddie got up and went to the water cooler in the corner of the room. He pulled a paper cup from the stack.

"I never heard of the name Rufus Davenport," he said. "To box you have to register. The Boxing Federation will give you a license. They print a list I know backward. Not only in this state but in most of the others."

He poured water into a cup and raised it. Like he was offering me some. I put up a hand to mean no. Eddie drank the water and threw the empty cup in a trash can.

"Could he fight under another name?" I asked.

Eddie went back to his chair.

"Maybe," he said. "But I haven't met a boxer yet who doesn't want to see his name in headlines. Anonymity. It's for writers. Poets. People like that. Not fighters."

"But it is possible?" I said. "He could be Bombshell Baxter? Hollywood Maninsky?"

Eddie raised an eyebrow.

"Possible but unlikely," he said. "I'll check with an old southpaw who hangs around the gyms. Barney Bates. He drops by here from time to time. He might know something."

There was a clock on the wall behind where he was standing. It reminded me I was on a meter.

"Something else," I said and fished in my pants for

some loose change. "The Cuban kid punching the bag. He needs to work on his lower body."

Eddie stared at me.

"Tell him to run the five blocks to where I parked my Chevy and thumb change into the slot. He's got three minutes."

TWELVE

Harry Drives to the Four Aces Casino

An hour later I was crawling north to Sunny Isles Beach in a long line of slow-moving traffic. I had no idea if Rufus Davenport could fight like he said. I only knew his name wasn't registered. Six kids need a lot of everything. His salary would be stretched. Every extra cent would help. A jade bracelet would mean a lot of extra cents.

But Rufus Davenport wasn't the only suspect.

My next stop was Maria's good brother. From him I needed to find out more about the bad one. And the truth about Maria.

Halfway to the Four Aces Casino I realized I was far too early. Casinos catered to the night trade. Gambling and dining. If I showed up now the only people there would be cleaners and telephone receptionists. I took my foot off the gas and poked the nose of my Chevy in the direction of Milton's Deli.

The place was full. Everyone in town. Eating. Talking. Not a seat anywhere. Milton put me in his office. I sat at the table he used for a desk and ordered strawberry cheesecake with a glass of lemon tea. And I also said that I needed to use the phone. Milton told me he couldn't remember a time when I didn't and to help myself.

While he was out of the room I called directory assistance. The voice on the end of the line gave me the number of the Four Aces Casino and thanked me for using the service. I dialed what I had written down.

Reception answered at once. I learned that Diego began his shift at eight. He would work until two in the morning with a half hour break at around eleven. I made a note of it.

Milton came back and placed my order in front of me.

"Did you hear about Benny Rosen?" he asked as I took a bite into a fresh strawberry. The fruit was sweet. Fat and full of juice.

"I should have heard something?" I said.

Milton made a face. A face like I should have heard.

"He is redecorating his store."

"I never knew."

"He put a sign in the window."

I sipped tea.

"So?"

"'Business Bad as Usual During Alterations.'"

"Benny all over," I said.

Someone called to Milton from the counter for an ice cream soda. I paid my tab, wished Milton mazel tov, and headed off for the Four Aces Casino.

I took my time. I had plenty. Eight o'clock was still way off.

I drove with the top down and let the fresh air get to my face. With a cooling wind and the calm light of a Florida nightfall, it felt good to be working. Who else works at eighty-seven? From choice. Not working to pay for a prostate operation or your brother-in-law's funeral. Give up? I'll tell you. A Supreme Court judge. An orchestra conductor. A Jewish comedian. And Harry Lipkin.

I drove steadily and fiddled around with the radio for some music to fit my mood.

I found Benny Goodman. His trio from the thirties. "China Boy." Fast as a Ferrari and crisp as a new deck of cards. Piano. Drums and clarinet. They made history. Whites and blacks appearing on the same stage. Teddy Wilson. Gene Krupa and Benny on the stick. Correction. Two Jews and a black. I tapped my finger on the rim of the steering wheel and I thought about my life back then. Not a worry in the world. I drank a little. I shot craps. I met dames with big smiles and no plans for the future. Then came Hitler. I joined the Marines. Hitler's show closed and they put me on a troop ship home. After a year looking for work I got a job with the Miami Police Department. After three years I'd had enough of shift work and routine. I quit being a cop and took out a Private Investigator's license. It's been one hell of a game. And the hundred-dollar bill in my pocket said I was still in it.

The flashing candy pink and lemon neon sign for the Four Aces was right ahead of me. I nosed the Chevy along the narrow well-kept drive that led to the parking lot and got out. I took in a lungful of the evening air and coughed it back out and let my feet carry me to the staff entrance. It was eight on the dot. Time to meet Diego Lopez.

THIRTEEN

Harry Meets Diego Lopez

The security guard was one up from sumo size in a brown uniform with a yellow and red company badge in the shape of a shield sewn onto the left breast pocket. He wore dark glasses to cover his eyes, a peaked cap to cover his head, and a .44 Magnum in a holster on a strap to keep the top of his pants from bursting.

I held my license under his nose.

"I made an appointment," I said. "To see Diego Lopez."

He didn't read my ID. Or get up from his seat. He just waved his hand like it was the toughest job he'd had all day.

"Last door on your right, bud," he mumbled. "It says, no entry, keep out, private, staff only."

I put my license back in my pocket and went to the

door as directed. I gave a polite knock and pushed it open.

The room was brightly lit with a row of lockers on one side and a mirror running the length of the wall on the other. Under the mirror was a tabletop. The kind you see in theater dressing rooms. About thirty men were getting ready for work. Grooming their hair and fixing their bow ties. Most were young Hispanics. Young men with charming smiles and gentle manners. They all had their name, photo, and signature on a plastic card fixed to a ribbon round their neck. I looked for one that said Diego Lopez.

Maria's older brother was at the far end of the room trimming a thick black mustache. I sat on an empty stool beside him.

"I am Harry Lipkin," I said. "I need a few minutes of your time."

He snipped a couple of hairs.

"A few minutes is all I got," he said. "I'm due on the floor."

"It's about a theft," I told him. "At the house where your sister works."

He put the scissors down and picked up a bottle of aftershave.

"I never been there."

"Your sister sends money home," I said. "She says your father is sick and your older sister is looking after him."

Diego Lopez rubbed limes and spices onto his skin.

"We both send money home," he said.

"And your brother, Manuel?" I asked.

"What about him?"

"Does he send money home?"

Diego Lopez stood up and got into a black vest decorated with gold and red aces.

"My brother is awaiting trial," he said. "Auto theft. Five counts."

"No kidding," I said and took out my notebook. "Care to flesh it out some?"

"You know the cost of bail," Lopez said. "Figure it out yourself."

I wrote it down. All of it. In big letters.

"How long before he stands trial?"

Maria's brother ran a comb through his thick hair.

"Next week. Next year. They don't say."

Men dressed for work were already heading for the door that led to the casino's gambling deck. I checked my watch.

"And Maria," I said. "Anything else you think I should know?"

He came close and stared at me with hard black eyes.

"Forget all about my sister," he said. "Or you might end up in a lot of trouble."

"Is that a threat, Mr. Lopez?" I asked.

"Friendly advice," he replied and slipped a pair of silver bands over his shirt sleeves.

His arms were short and thickset. No fat. Just muscle. His build was flyweight. Some men get soft and flabby spending their nights dealing cards and spinning roulette wheels. Most men. But not Diego Lopez. He was a man whose advice would be worth listening to.

Outside the casino the security guard was eating a pizza as big as a circus ring. The empty box was on the floor. Next to it were three others. I climbed back into my Chevy and drove through the indigo dusk back to Warmheart. Cruising along the highway I thought about Maria the maid and Diego the card dealer. I had them as a couple of honest hardworking Bolivians. Full of heart and good intentions. But a bad brother might just change that. It wasn't time to put a pencil line through the name of Maria Lopez.

Not yet.

FOURTEEN

Harry Gets Some More Messages

It was after eleven when I got back to Samuel Gompers Avenue. I put the Chevy back in the garage and entered the house through the front door. On the way to the kitchen I noticed that the red light was blinking on my answering machine in the office. I let it blink. I was hungry. I heated a can of chicken soup and poured it into a bowl. Then I took it into the office and checked my calls while eating.

There were three calls. The first was the message from Mrs. Weinberger. The one I'd heard earlier. The second was also from Mrs. Weinberger. Another expensive piece of jewelry had been stolen.

"From under my very nose. A diamond-encrusted gold brooch that my late husband gave me. It was a birthday present. From Van Cleef and Arpels. In the shape of a lotus leaf. The most

wonderful piece of jewelry you have ever seen. Taken from me like the jade I called about this morning that you never called me back about. Are you ill that you can't answer the phone? Has something happened to you? God forbid. Please, Mr. Lipkin. Call me as soon as you get this message."

I looked at my watch. Too late again. I gulped some soup. Not bad for a can. Nice and salty. Not too many hard bits. Dentures do so hate hard bits.

I pressed the button for the third message. It was from Eddie Berkowitz.

"News, Harry. Barney Bates dropped by the gym an hour after you left. He saw Rufus Davenport fight in South Florida. A month ago. But the name he boxed under was Frank Dunlop. He said that he hit hard and hit the target. It bothered him. The man in the ring had class and with class he should have a reputation. Yet Barney had never heard of Frank Dunlop until that night. After the fight he spoke to the promoter over a beer. That's how he found out. The promoter let it slip. Frank Dunlop is Rufus Davenport. One and the same."

I wrote it all down. But why the alias? Eddie was right. Boxers crave fame as well as a purse. I could think of only one reason. Rufus didn't want it to get around that he boxed and drove for Mrs. Weinberger. Fighting has a bad reputation. Chauffeuring doesn't.

I took my empty soup bowl into the kitchen and put it in the sink. It was a very old Lithuanian china soup bowl that had once belonged to my Great-Aunt Mimi. It was white with blue figures in national dress dancing in the middle and flowers round the rim. There had been six bowls once. This was the last. I washed it carefully and placed it to drain.

It was time to sleep. But first I took my notebook from my jacket pocket and went back into the office. I sat at my desk, looked at what I had so far and the schedule I had planned for the next few days. I'd talk to Oscar Letto to check out Mr. Lee. Oscar had spent his life at Gulfstream. First, feeding ponies. Then riding them and now training them.

As for Amos and his New Jerusalem, Rabbi Katz might know something. I'd call him.

Steve was the easy one. Any dope dealer within a mile of Mr. Weinberger's garden would give me a lead.

News that Rufus Davenport was on the level meant his name was getting close to dropping off the list. But only close. Boxing is no guarantee of an extra payday. Not like the price of an antique carved-jade bracelet. For the time being he'd keep his place with the others.

I'd just turned off the desk light when the phone rang. Outside my office window the full moon was sitting on a palm tree and turned the light in my room pure silver.

I picked up the receiver.

"Good evening, Mrs. Weinberger."

There was a pause.

"How did you know it's me?"

"I got a sixth sense. You can't do my job without it."

"Why didn't you call me? I left two messages."

"I thought you might be in bed already."

"I am in bed already. I've been in bed for two hours."

"You can't sleep?"

"Yes. I can't sleep. The thought that a person in this house is stealing my precious belongings . . ."

She sobbed.

"Someone I employ and trust, Mr. Lipkin. It is horrible. Horrible."

She sobbed some more.

"Mr. Lipkin, have you any idea who is doing this to me? Any idea at all?"

"Sure. I got lots of ideas, but that's all they are. I got nothing solid. Not yet. In a few more days I'll have a clearer picture."

"Please hurry. It is making me feel so vulnerable. No one here to comfort me. Knowing the person I turn to might well be the thief."

"The fact that he or she has stolen from you again this evening narrows the field."

Mrs. Weinberger blew her nose.

"Cold comfort, Mr. Lipkin."

"I will call as soon as I make some headway. Rest assured. We'll nail them."

There was a long silence. I could hear a clock close to her strike twelve.

"Thank you for being so understanding, Mr. Lipkin. You are a real gentleman if you don't mind me saying."

"I don't mind you saying."

She gave a small laugh. Maybe to reassure herself. Maybe for some other reason. It was the kind of laugh she would have given someone when she looked like Doris Day with dark hair. She'd give it to someone she was maybe fond of.

We both said good night.

Then I hung up and went to bed. Sleep took no time at all.

· FIFTEEN ·

Harry Meets Oscar Letto

round two in the morning it started to rain. With most of the roof tiles that covered my bedroom on the grass in my yard it didn't take long for water to drop from the ceiling. It wasn't Niagara Falls but it was enough to force me out of bed. I grabbed some bedding and headed for the living room couch. So far the rain hadn't made it to the living room.

A couch. Any couch. Even a couch that cost a thousand dollars from Bergdorf Goodman is not a place for an old man to sleep. Read a book maybe. Watch TV. Pet a dog. But not sleep. Old feet get cold quick and covers on a couch never stay covers for long. They somehow climb up your legs and expose your feet. Your feet freeze. Most of the time the covers just fall onto the floor. Then you freeze all over.

When the clock said four I finally quit trying to sleep.

I decided to drive down to Gulfstream instead. I took a shower and got dressed. Then I made some black coffee and drank it with a toasted waffle covered in cream cheese. It was six o'clock. I called Oscar and told him I was on my way over to see him. I said I needed information about a butler called Lee. He told me he'd be waiting once he was through giving Sadie's Sweetheart a workout.

Oscar trained Thoroughbreds. Sadie's Sweetheart was the latest in a long line. She was class. Six listed races. Six straight wins. He named the filly after his mother. Sadie Letto. Good stock was how Oscar described his mother. A woman well bred.

It took an hour from Warmheart to Letto's Stables. Most days it's more but that early the traffic was light. From the highway I drove along the narrow road that ran through the meadows surrounding ten miles of open land overlooking the ocean. Some days Oscar would take his horses to the beach and train them on the sand. A lot of people would go and watch. Other trainers. Interested parties who were aiming to copy his methods. They looked and hoped to learn. But no matter how hard they tried they never came close. And high-class horse traders who couldn't copy Oscar tried to buy him. He got offers from all over. The Saudis. The Irish. The Brits. The French. Every breeder with a stable full of Thoroughbred nags wanted him. Oscar got more offers from royal families through his mailbox than I got handbills from the Chinese carryout. But all they got back was a no thanks but thanks for asking. Oscar Letto was a Miami boy. All four foot nine of him. Happy with what he had.

I parked in the lot in front of the main stables and looked around for a horse. If there was a horse there was a good chance Oscar would be sitting on it. I found him in the time it takes to stub your toe in the dark.

"Good to see you, Harry," Oscar called down from the saddle.

"Likewise," I shouted back.

He was in one of his famous outfits. The kind that earned him the name Dandy back in the days he rode professionally. Pink silk top. Purple breeches. Orange hat with lemon-yellow polka dots. Your wouldn't miss Oscar Letto dressed to whip a nag round a track. Not unless he was standing behind a bar stool.

"Give me a couple of minutes," Oscar said. "First off. I need to put Sadie in a blanket. She cools down too fast for her own good. You want to tag on my tail?"

I got out of the Chevy and followed him to a row of stables where a girl in blue denims and rubber boots was waiting. She had red hair cut short and plenty of freckles. Her eyes were sea green. Oscar climbed down and gave her his mount.

"Sally," he said and nodded in my direction. "My old pal, Harry Lipkin."

Sally smiled. She didn't speak. She didn't have to. Her smile was enough.

Oscar rubbed a hand over the filly's flank and looked at the frothy sweat his fingers picked up.

"Check her shoes," Oscar told the girl. "She eased up a mile out."

Sally led Sadie's Sweetheart into a stall with a star painted in gold above the open doors. Oscar looked at the sky. Sniffed the air. There was a rumble of thunder somewhere close. Out at sea. Somewhere over Biscayne.

"Rain on the way," he said. "Let's talk in my office."

It was a big room with a view overlooking the stone cobbled yard and two rows of stables. The decor didn't get much beyond a full-size oil painting of Oscar on a horse.

We both found a place to sit. I took the sofa. Oscar sank back into his black leather desk chair.

"You mentioned a butler earlier," he said. "A man called Lee."

"An Asian. Chinese. Speaks like an Englishman."

"Your client?"

"He's employed by my client," I replied. "When Mr. Lee isn't on duty he spends his time at Gulfstream."

Oscar folded his arms. "That's not a crime, Harry."

"No," I said. "But theft is. Someone is stealing from my client and almost certainly selling the goods for cash. My guess is they need it to feed some kind of habit. Or pay for some kind of hobby. Lee is a suspect. He told me he makes gambling pay. I need your help to prove it's true. And if it is, how much he makes."

Oscar Letto thought about it.

"Ten thousand to win a thousand. That's how a pro operates, Harry. To make a lot of money, Mr. Lee would first need to have a lot of money."

I took out my notebook. But I didn't make a note. I let Oscar carry on talking. He might just say something new.

"Couldn't he have been born lucky?" I asked. "Like you get born to sing like Perry Como? Or have eyes like Ava Gardner?"

He shook his head.

"Gambling is a job, Harry. You know it. I know it. A pro only bets on information. And pros pay for it. They pay plenty."

"Then Mr. Lee has someone on the inside?"

"A punter wins on one race in twenty," he said. "The Racing Commission publishes the figures once a year. But an average is an average. Punters can go years without a break. Take it from me, Harry. To make his trips to the track pay, the butler has to have information. And it will be hot and expensive. There's no other way."

The phone on his desk rang. Oscar Letto answered it.

"On my way," he said. "I put a worksheet out. Tell him to look at Sadie first."

He hung up. Then got to his feet. I did the same.

"The vet is here to do his rounds," Oscar said. "I got to go. Give me a day or two, Harry. I'll ask the guys who operate the track. If an Asian is picking up a lot of cabbage on a regular basis, they are sure to know. As soon as I hear something I'll call you."

On my way back to the Chevy rain began falling once more. And falling heavy. I thought about driving home and getting into something to keep me dry. A raincoat. A hat. Gumshoes. But home was a distance. Coral Gables was just around the corner. And besides, I owed Mrs. Weinberger another visit.

· S I X T E E N ·

Harry Reports Back to Mrs. Weinberger

The rain had stopped by the time I got to the Weinberger property. The sky to the east was breaking up and streaks of blue were beginning to show between the drifting gray clouds. I took my toe off the gas and pulled by a row of fruit trees in bloom. The heavy rain had torn away most of the petals and the soggy path beneath was the pink and white of a strawberry milkshake. Steve would soon be busy with a broom.

I checked the knot in my necktie and rang the bell and waited while Mr. Lee hotfooted it along the corridor. He opened the door and lifted an eyebrow.

"I wasn't aware that Mrs. Weinberger was expecting you," he said.

"She isn't," I told him. "I was passing and thought I'd drop by. There are a few more questions I need to ask."

He led me to the patio.

"I will inform Mrs. Weinberger you are here," the butler said. "May I get you some refreshment while you wait?"

"Coffee," I said. "Black. Strong. I need a lift. Up most of the night. Out early. Down at the track. Talking to Oscar Letto. One hell of a guy. Natty outfits. Fast nags. A onetime top jockey. He trains bloodstock. You must know him."

His expression did that thing again. It went dark. Like when a black cloud is blown across the sun. Then the cloud moved on.

"Not a name I am familiar with," he said and glided back into the house.

I looked around for a seat.

The pool was ready for the day. Someone had arranged the loungers and put up the umbrellas. They had swept away the rain and cleared away empty glasses from low tables. My guess was it would have been Maria. I eased into a comfortable pile of thick cushions. Under the warm sun my eyelids gradually lost control. I couldn't blame them. They had been through a night without sleep. They had opened real early. And they were old eyelids. Sleep-hungry eyelids. I tried to keep them from closing. The more I tried to keep them open the more they forced themselves shut. Finally they dropped down over my eyes and sent me drifting pleasantly into the harmless land of noonday dreams. It was Mrs. Weinberger's voice that opened them.

"Good morning, Mr. Lipkin," she said. "This is an unexpected but very pleasant surprise."

I sat up fast as I could and almost killed a yawn.

"You looked so peaceful," she continued. "I asked myself, wouldn't it be kinder to let Mr. Lipkin snooze a little longer?"

She was wearing slacks and a turquoise tunic with a drawstring tie. A ton of colored beads hung in rows round her neck and there were some more on her wrists. She was holding a wide-brimmed straw hat.

"I don't usually snooze this early," I said. "The rain kept me awake. It came in through the place I once had tiles. You saw them on the lawn the day you hired me. You remember?"

Her lips said yes but the rest of her said she didn't. She looked at me. Blank. Then she looked at the stacked tray.

"I see Maria has brought you some coffee," she said. "Let me pour you a cup."

I let her.

"I couldn't sleep much either," she confessed and handed me the java. "I kept thinking about my stolen brooch."

I took a sip and felt caffeine hit the dead spots. One or two came back to life.

"I need some confidential information about the method you use to pay your staff," I said and took out my notebook. "If you find it difficult talking over your financial arrangements I fully understand. But it will help me a lot if you can."

Mrs. Weinberger perched on the edge of the lounger facing me.

"I just want this whole business over with, Mr. Lipkin. Feel free to ask me anything you want."

I made it as short and simple as I knew how.

"From what I have picked up so far all your staff have ways of spending more than they earn," I said. "The chef is raising money for Jews in Ethiopia. Maria has a sick father. Mr. Lee plays the ponies. Your gardener smokes grass as well as cutting it. And Rufus Davenport has too many kids. If a member of your staff banks a check it is a relatively simple matter to establish if they are in the black. If they are in the black there's no big reason to steal as well as work."

The sun was high now. Hot. Noon. The hottest time of day. Norma Weinberger put on her sombrero. It suited her. Mexican women. Jewish women. Dark hair. Dark eyes.

"I've never discussed their private lives with them," she said. "They get paid on the last day of every month. If they worked for my neighbor Mrs. Silverman they'd get a lot less than they get here. I know that for a fact."

There was nothing on Norma Weinberger's feet apart from varnish. On her toes. Magenta varnish. Fresh. I could smell the acetate. She looked down at her toes. They were drying nicely.

"I need to know if you pay the butler and his pals by a check or with cash," I said. "Please understand. It is important."

"I can't see why, Mr. Lipkin," she said. "As far as I am concerned they get paid. That is all that matters. What difference does it make how I pay them? A check or cash?"

"Because the trail cash leaves is tougher to follow than a check's," I said.

There was a short silence. Then I went into detail.

"When I want information from a bank all I have to do is to look at a sheet of printed paper," I told her. "But a pocket full of dimes takes time to trace. A lot of time. You use it meeting a lot of the right people. Sure. Sometimes you get lucky. Sometimes you can get as much information from a teller at the pari-mutuel as you can from a clerk behind the bulletproof glass in the First Bank of Florida. The longer it takes the more you pay me. And the greater the chance more of your stuff will get stolen. *Farshtayn?*"

Apart from the one word of Yiddish she didn't understand any of it. She didn't have to. All my client needed to know was that Harry Lipkin was onto something. But I was still in the dark about how she paid the salaries. I gave it to her no frills.

"Cash or check, Mrs. Weinberger? I want an answer. I need it to know what I am to do from here on."

Mrs. Weinberger took off her hat and fanned her face with the brim.

"I pay cash for everything, Mr. Lipkin. I always have. I know that it is more common to use a credit card, or a check. But not me. With cash, I know where I am. I have a cash box for housekeeping. A cash box for personal expenses. A cash box for just about everything."

"And there is, I assume, one for paying the staff?"

"As you say, Mr. Lipkin."

I drank what remained of the coffee and stood up. Mrs. Weinberger did likewise. In bare feet her head was level with the knot in my tie.

"What you told me has been a big help," I said. "Now I can plan my next move."

We were standing close. Closer than at any time before. I could smell her sunblock and the hint of perfume Elizabeth Arden put in the cherry wax she'd run so carefully over her lips.

"I trust you, Mr. Lipkin," she said. "Trust is a rare word for me to say."

I left a pause.

"A rare word for me to hear, Mrs. Weinberger."

Her hand moved to mine. Close. Very close. But stopped short of touching.

SEVENTEEN

Steve Threatens Harry

Steve was by my Impala. He was holding a plastic sack and a spade. He waited until I had got into my seat. Then he bent down and talked through the open window.

"I hear you been hard at work," he said.

His voice didn't sound quite so Mr. Tambourine Man.

"Only doing what I've been paid to," I said.

"Sticking your nose in where it don't belong."

"Investigating a crime. It's my business, remember?"

"Snooping."

"You shovel up dead petals. I find thieves. Each to his own."

Steve stuck his face close to mine.

"Snooping can get a guy into a lot of trouble," he said. "The kind of trouble they got no cure for."

"Trouble," I said and laughed at him. "Don't tell me

about trouble. Jews invented it. We're still here. All thirteen million. And I am still here. Alive and kicking."

Steve ran a finger over the edge of his spade.

"If you want to keep it that way," he said, "take some advice from Steve. Ask your questions someplace else."

There is only one reply a private eye can give that kind of advice. It's on page one of the manual *How to Become a Successful Private Investigator.*

"And if I don't?" I asked.

He looked at the spade. Then he looked at me.

"A grave takes no time to dig," he said. "Soft earth. The kind you find in a wood where no one goes. A deep hole takes no time at all."

I let him think he'd put a scare in me. Just for the kick of it. Then I gave him the hardest look a man of my age can give and pitched a scare back.

"You can't threaten an eighty-seven-year-old with death," I growled through my dentures. "Move me into a condo without an elevator. Maybe. Make me eat chicken soup without a bread roll. Certainly. But I got insurance. Not from Mutual of Omaha. I got it with me. In the glove compartment."

Steve watched as I opened the flap and searched through the bottles of pills. The out-of-town road maps. The machine I got for taking my blood pressure. The collection of big band jazz cassettes I play when there's nothing on the radio. The packet of mints. The screwdriver with interchangeable heads. The eight-by-ten black-and-white head shot of a man I was paid to trace ten years ago. The empty ballpoint pen.

"Stick around, Steve," I said. "My insurance is right in back. From Smith and Wesson of Massachusetts. Under the truss I used before I had my hernia fixed."

I pulled out the snub nose .38. The same as I keep in my desk drawer. And I waved it at Steve.

"There are six slugs in the chamber," I said. "Fat and happy slugs. Waiting for a body to hole up in."

Steve stared at the muzzle pointing at his chest and dropped the spade.

"Now beat it," I said. "Old fingers get tired quick and this thing I'm pointing at your heart might just decide to go off."

Steve beat it. Fast. Fast as a man with a drug habit can.

Then I put life in my Chevy and drove home.

· EIGHTEEN ·

Harry Has an Unexpected Visitor

had just turned off the Dixie Highway and was about fifteen minutes from Warmheart when I noticed the black Maserati Bellagio in my rearview mirror. When I slowed down it slowed down. When I picked up speed it picked up speed. There was too much of a gap between us for me to see the driver and even if the car had been right behind it would have made no difference. The windows were tinted.

I reached home and pulled up beside the curb. As I did my tail accelerated and cut in front. Emergency brakes got pulled. Tires squealed. Engines got turned off. The passenger door swung open and a kid jumped out. He moved quickly. Without speaking he pulled me from my seat and rammed something hard into the base of my spine. Just under the spot where I get the ache in the morning. The ache that doctors can't figure out.

"Walk," he said. "And don't try nothing funny. From here I can't miss. This heater in your lumber stack can blow a hole in you big enough to drive an elephant through."

I laughed. To myself. Just a little and not too long.

"You've been watching too many late-night crime drama repeats," I said. "Gangster talk."

"Save it, cop," he snarled. "I'll tell you when to cough."

We reached the door.

"Open up, cop," the kid ordered. "Make it snappy."

I took the keys carefully from my jacket pocket and opened the door.

We went inside. Me first. The kid behind. Close enough behind to feel his breath on the back of my neck.

"We need someplace we can talk," he said. "You got someplace nice and quiet?"

"I got an office," I said.

"Show me."

I showed him. Once inside he took the nose of his gun from my ninth vertebra and stepped back a pace.

"Turn around, cop," he said. "And no tricks."

I turned around without tricks. Tricks were for younger men. I looked him over.

He was early twenties. Slender frame with a black suit and a black porkpie hat. His shirt was black and so was his tie. He wore expensive shades that had reflecting glass and his shoes looked handmade. They were black. I couldn't see his socks but my guess was they weren't chocolate and yellow diamond check. The pistol he was pointing at me was a Springfield Armory semiautomatic. Even a near miss would kill you.

"I don't know who you are or what you are doing here," I said. "And I am not a cop. I was a cop. Sixty years ago. Now I work private."

The kid came close. "Once a cop, always a cop."

We were going around in circles.

"Listen," I said. "I have no powers of arrest. I am not paid by the good citizens of Miami to enforce the law. I am paid by private citizens to investigate minor offenses that cops can't be bothered with. These kinds of offenses are usually the work of bad citizens. But not always. Some are made by just stupid citizens. There are some instances when a minor offense might lead to or involve crimes that require the police. Like if someone gets murdered or kidnapped. But normally I do my job and the police do theirs. We don't mix unless we have to."

There was silence.

While the kid tried to put together what I told him I moved cautiously to the window and looked at the view. A fatter and older version of the kid was sitting on the hood of the Maserati. He was casually smoking a cigarette and staring at the sky.

"That's just your story," the kid said finally.

I went to my desk and sat down.

"You want to tell me what you want?" I said. "My guess

is you have something on your mind. And me being a cop or not being a cop has nothing to do with it."

The kid took a corner of the desk and perched. He inched the brim of his hat up his forehead with the tip of his gun.

"Steve," he said.

"Steve?" I said.

"Steve," he said.

"Allen? McQueen? A lot of Steves."

The kid released the safety catch on the gun. The single click sounded loud as a small-town church clock chiming one.

"Tattoos and a shovel," the kid said. "Digs up weeds for a broad called Weinberger. Her man in the day. Our man nights."

"You got a garden?" I asked. "Must be one hell of a job trimming a shrub in the dark."

The kid flinched but let it go.

"We supply goods. Luxury goods," he drawled. "The kind of luxury goods you can't buy over the counter. Most of our clients pay on the nail. We make them happy. They make us happy. But there are some who forget. Steve reminds them."

"And how does Steve do that exactly?" I said. "Stick a centipede down their shirt?"

The kid used a finger to mime a blade cutting his cheek. And then his throat.

"They remember," he said.

It was now beginning to make some kind of sense. The price of Steve's habit was written off against his job as a part-time debt collector for the black mafia.

Outside the sky was quickly clouding over. The storm that had spent the night over my roof was on its way back. And fast. Suddenly the sky was full of thunder. Rain began falling. Heavily.

The kid looked at his gun. Then at me. Even under the reflecting glass of his shades I knew his eyes. Cold. Small. Hard. A killer's eyes.

I wondered what next. But not for long. There was a blast on the horn from the Maserati.

"Gotta go, cop," the kid said and slipped the gun into the holster inside his jacket. "Urgent business I got to take care of downtown."

"Pity," I said. "I was about to boil a kettle."

"Keep it boiling, cop," he said. "I'll be back real soon."

The kid waved to the driver from the window that he was on his way and took off down the passage.

I went to where the kid had been standing. I could only partly see the Maserati or the driver. But I could see the kid clearly. The room I use as an office extends up the front yard. When you look out the window you can see back down the yard to the porch as well as look out onto the street. I saw him open the front door and yell at the driver to get moving. I saw him slam the door back in the frame. Slam it hard. Much too hard. The walls each side of the door shook. The passage walls next to them shook. The whole house shook. The shaking dislodged the few tiles that were still in place. There was a row of about a dozen clinging to the ridge. One broke loose and began slipping down the sharp incline of the slippery rain-soaked beams. With each foot the tile picked up speed. Others followed. One after the other. Gray slate tiles that weigh just over a pound and a half with edges worn thin as a blade by the salt air from the Atlantic. Tiles traveling fast as a javelin is thrown fell from the roof onto the sodden yard. One after the other. Like axe heads. One fell exactly into the path where the kid was running. Neck high. Fast. Sharp. It sliced his head clean off. A kosher butcher's cleaver couldn't have done a neater job.

If I hadn't seen it I wouldn't have thought it possible. Like when you read *Ripley's Believe It or Not.* The sleepwalker who crossed the Gobi Desert. The cow that gave birth to a koala bear. But the evidence was there. The kid's head one place. The rest of him someplace else.

And I wasn't the only witness.

The Maserati crackled into life. Backed up. Spun in a half circle and accelerated out of sight down Samuel Gompers Avenue. Zero to eighty in four seconds.

I picked up the phone and dialed 911.

NINETEEN

Lieutenant Voss Questions Harry

The voice on the other end of the line told me I was speaking to Police Officer Loretta Gibbs. She asked who was calling and how she could help?

I gave my name and said that a young man in my front yard had been involved in a fatal accident. She took my address and said someone would be there in twenty minutes. A fatal accident didn't bother her. The how did it happen? The who was involved? The where was it? Those questions would be answered by someone in another department.

I thanked Loretta Gibbs for her time and hung up.

It was still raining. Not hard. But enough. I put on my hat and raincoat and went out to the yard and looked over the kid's cadaver.

His head was a few feet from his neck. His hat and glasses were just as they were when he put them on. I bent over his torso and took the gun and put it in my pocket. Then I searched him all over. There were a dozen small packets of cocaine wrapped in aluminum foil in his jacket pocket. These I also took. In another pocket was a small leather book of first names with codes next to them. The kid's wallet had only money. A couple of hundred in bills. No ID. No credit cards. No dry cleaning ticket. No pieces of paper to tell you who he was. And no cell. Nothing to link him to others. The kid was a pro. I replaced the wallet in his inside breast pocket and took the leather book, the drugs, and the gun back to the office.

The trick was to sell the Police Department a dummy. I didn't want them poking around into my case. But it wouldn't be easy. An accident? A tile? Off the roof? Sure. Mr. Lipkin. Be sensible. Come clean. I could hear it all. Like I told the kid. Sixty years ago I asked the same questions.

I needed a whole new script.

I put the kid's things in the wall safe I kept out of sight with a framed print of a flamenco dancer. Then I went to the bookshelf and pulled down the Bible from my collection of religious books. The other two were a hardback copy of *Exodus* signed by Leon Uris I picked up in a thrift store on Bayshore Drive while I was down there for a checkup at Mercy Hospital and Betty Grable's biography. *The Girl with the Million Dollar Legs*. One day I'd read it as well as look at the pictures.

The Bible wasn't a purchase. Not like the other books. It was a gift. More than a gift. Forced on me by a former client. Ralph J. Rawlston. Ralph was a salesman for DuPont and a devout Christian. Mostly a devout Christian. He wanted me to find out what his wife, Mona, did when he was on the road. Ralph suspected her of having an affair with the president of the local Lions Club. He also wanted me to know that by reading the Holy Word of God as proclaimed by His Only Son Made Flesh, not only would my Soul be Saved from Sin but I would have Life Eternal.

It was time I put the Almighty's Word to the test.

I went back outside and found that the rain had eased off to a light drizzle. I took the shades and hat off the kid's head and placed the Bible under his left arm. Then I made a final check that there was nothing to identify him. There was nothing that I could see. The labels on his suit and shirt and the rest of his outfit were designer names but not exclusive. You couldn't trace the owner by them. There were no obvious marks. No signs of a medical history. Satisfied the kid was clean I went back to my office and waited for the police.

The meat wagon arrived a few seconds before the squad car. Two men in protective clothes took a stretcher from the ambulance and two others began rigging up a plastic fence around the kid's head and body. A photographer climbed out of the squad car and began snapping.

He was followed by a uniformed officer and a detective in plainclothes. The detective gave the kid's head and body a quick once-over and strolled to the porch. He didn't need to ring the bell. I was ready for him.

"Harry Lipkin," I said. "It was me who made the call."

The plainclothes flashed his badge.

"Lieutenant Voss. Miami Police. Mind if I come in?"

I led him into the office and offered a seat. Voss sat down. He pulled a crumpled pack of Camels from his pocket, stuck half a cigarette in the corner of his mouth, and set light to it. I took the chair near the window.

He was short and heavy round the middle. His graying hair needed cutting. His tie needed a press and his shirt needed a wash. Needy. He had deep lines sunk into his forehead and his pale blue eyes told me that there wasn't much he hadn't seen apart from retirement.

"Tell it as it happened," Voss said and blew out smoke.

"There isn't a lot."

"As much as you can remember," Voss said.

"The young man called to give me the word of Jesus," I said. "It was raining hard so I asked him inside. A shelter from the storm."

"When was this?"

"About an hour ago."

Voss looked around for an ashtray. There wasn't one. He let me know with a look. I got up. Shuffled into the kitchen. Found a saucer with a crack that I didn't mind getting ash on and shuffled back to the office. I placed it on the arm of Voss's chair and sat back down.

Voss tapped ash into the saucer.

"Let me get this straight," he said. "You get a knock. It's a door stepper selling Jesus. You invite him and he gives you the spiel."

"Here one minute. Gone the next."

"What did you talk about?"

"He talked," I said. "I listened. It was about the Lord Jesus."

Voss sucked in some more smoke and let it out in a long stream.

"There's a mezuzah on your front doorframe," he said. "Only a Jew puts a prayer rolled up in a tube by the place he goes in and out."

"A lot of Jews live in Warmheart," I said. "People around here are mostly Semitic. There are around thirty thousand at a guess."

"Including Harry Lipkin?"

"Including Harry Lipkin."

He thought about it. Let me think about it. Took in more smoke and let more smoke out.

"So what was a Christian selling Jesus doing talking to you?"

I shrugged.

"Beats me, Lieutenant," I said. "Maybe the young man figured I was ripe for conversion. Jews do. Convert. Sometimes. Not many. One in a million. Maybe two. Three at most."

Voss stared at me hard. To say otherwise he would have had to have been there. Seen for himself. He left it to one side and carried on with the routine.

"Did you see the accident?" he asked. There was a heavy emphasis on the word "accident."

"Unfortunately." I said. "I saw him to the door and we shook hands. He was standing just outside the porch. He was telling me that Jesus would always be there for us when lightning hit the roof. The tiles came down and he took one. It hit him direct."

I put my hand to my neck to show. "Right here."

The lieutenant killed his cigarette and got to his feet.

"That will be all for now, Mr. Lipkin," he said, looking down at me. "I will have to wait for the pathologist's report before I do anything else. As it stands I suspect it will read accidental death. But in the meantime I would ask you not to leave town without letting me know."

"No plans to leave town," I said and let Voss find his own way out.

Then I took the saucer to the kitchen and emptied the dead butt into the trash can. It was time for a snack.

I filled a bagel with lox and cream cheese, drank a glass of lemon tea, and gave some thought to the day so far. Progress yet. For a start my hunch about Steve fooling around with narcotics was now a fact. He paid for his habit working part-time for a drug-dealing army of gun-toting pistoleros. Sure. He could have made extra robbing Mrs. Weinberger. She was a vulnerable woman and had plenty worth lifting. But finding a reliable fence is never easy. There is always a risk involved. The mob gave Steve steady work and offered protection.

I went back to the office and took my list of suspects from the file. I put just a light pencil line through Steve's name. So far I'd checked out Mr. Lee and I'd checked out Maria.

Amos was next.

TWENTY

Harry Tracks Down an Old Friend

Rabbi Lionel Rifkin married my cousin Ira's sister-in-law Pearl. Lionel often talked about the lost tribes of Israel. The Jews of Ethiopia were his speciality. If anyone knew about Ethiopian Jews in Miami it would be Rabbi Rifkin. The only problem was that we hadn't seen each other since Pearl's funeral. Five years ago. Or was it ten? He was ninety whenever it was.

The last place I knew for sure Rabbi Rifkin worked was the Beth Jacob. I dialed their number.

"My name is Ruby," a warm and helpful sounding voice said. "May I ask who is calling?"

"You most certainly may, Ruby," I replied. "My name is Harry Lipkin and I am trying to locate an old pal. Rabbi Lionel Rifkin. When I knew him he was working at the Beth Jacob. But that was some time ago. My guess is that he has possibly retired."

There was a pause while Ruby thought about it.

"I'm going to make some inquiries," Ruby said. "It might take a while. Miriam is out sick."

"Sorry to hear it," I said. "Who is Miriam?"

"Miriam is the person who would know about Rabbi Rifkin," Ruby explained. "Julie won't know any more than me."

"Julie?"

"Taken over for Miriam while she's sick. Would you please hold, Mr. Lipkin?"

"Happy to, Ruby," I said.

While the phone played what sounded like a banjo band version of Vivaldi's *Four Seasons* I killed time thinking about the Beth Jacob.

Meyer Lansky and his Murder Inc. mob went there in 1936. Local Jews called it the Gangster Schul. But Lansky wasn't bad all through. When the Nazis held rallies in New York and other big cities, Lansky's mob went and broke them up. They beat them with sticks and the hilts of pistols. Beat them till they bled. Lansky made those damn Nazis run.

When Ruby came back she had a number.

"Thank you for holding, Mr. Lipkin. Julie was no help. She had to ask Rabbi Cohen who then had to ask Rabbi Pressler who then asked Rabbi Greenhouse. Rabbi Greenhouse knew Rabbi Rifkin. Not well, but well enough to have a note of Rabbi Rifkin's last known residence. I have it right here. Are you ready to take it down?"

"All ears."

"Have you something to write with?"

"And to write on," I said.

Ruby spelled it out and I made a note. It was a Tampa exchange.

I thanked Ruby for her trouble and hung up. Then I called the number.

I didn't have to wait long before a recorded voice answered and gave me a choice of options and numbers to press. I pressed three. The concierge answered at once.

"You are through to the Heights Condominium. Mike speaking."

"My name is Harry Lipkin," I said. "I am trying to contact a rabbi called Rifkin. I have this as his residence."

"It was," Mike said. "Until six months ago. I am sorry to have to inform you that Rabbi Rifkin is currently hospitalized."

The news shook me.

"Is it bad?" I asked.

"I have no record," Mike replied. "But I can give you the name of the hospital and their contact details. They are on our database."

"I'll take them," I said. "If you would be so kind."

There was a minute while Mike checked on his computer. Then he came back on the line.

"Rabbi Rifkin is at the Mordecai Medical Center, in Sweetwater. The Association for the Health and Care of Retired Rabbis is the body looking after him. His room here has now been vacated and is occupied by another party."

There was a short pause. There was something on his mind. It was that kind of pause. I was right.

"I hope you don't take offense" Mike said. "But I have to ask the reason for your inquiry. It is a matter of routine, for security purposes only. We ask everyone who makes an inquiry such as yours."

"I am not offended," I told him. "I am looking for information. Specialist information. The kind that only someone like Rabbi Rifkin might be able to supply."

Mike listened. Put it someplace. The database probably.

"In what capacity?" Mike asked. "Sounds intriguing."

"I am a private detective," I said.

"A detective!" Mike almost choked. "How totally thrilling."

"A job," I said.

"But so dramatic. And believe me, I should know. I only do this part-time. I am actually a professional actor. Musical theater mainly. Did you see the *Singing Detective*? You must have. A lot of my friends thought it fabulous and of course it was, in a way, but I kept thinking to myself, Paul—that's my stage name, Paul, Paul Granger—there is a whole lot more you would have done with this if they had given it to you. I would have taken my motivation from trees in spring. Color. Light. Freshness. Do you know what I mean?"

There wasn't room for an answer.

"Anyway," Mike carried on. "They are doing a Stephen Sondheim season at the East Tampa Arts Center through the summer, and there is just a teeny-weeny chance I might get something. I would just love to do Sweeny Todd, or *Assassins,* or *A Little Night Music,* or anything, even a Rodgers and Hammerstein, *Oklahoma* is fabulous, better still, the lead role, Robert, in *Company.*"

I agreed that Mike would be just fabulous playing Robert and he gave me the phone number of the Mordecai Medical Center. I called it.

Reception confirmed that Rabbi Lionel Rifkin was a patient. I could visit him anytime between three in the afternoon and eight in the evening. I didn't need an appointment. I said I would be there in a couple of hours and got ready.

· TWENTY-ONE ·

Harry Drives to the Mordecai Medical Center

The traffic was flowing easily until I turned south onto the interstate, where it slowed almost to a standstill. Ahead I could see a number of police cars with flashing lights. Three lines of traffic were being merged into one. A highway sideshow.

Drivers in front of me were slowing down. Hoping to get a better look. At the point where we filed into a single lane there was plenty to see.

Men in bright yellow protective clothing and hard hats were sweeping broken glass and bits of metal to the side of the highway. A couple of medics were talking to each other and shaking their heads. A couple more were lifting a stretcher on wheels from the back of a meat wagon. Another was unwrapping a body bag. Cops were everywhere talking on cell phones. Giving orders. Taking orders. At the center was a team of firefighters with oxyacetylene torches. They were cutting the burned-out buckled shell of a black Italian coupe from the fender of a heavy-duty dump truck. If someone was laying odds on who built the car I'd take them. However short. Maserati.

With the show over I picked up speed and arrived at the Mordecai Medical Center in late afternoon. I parked in the lot they set aside for visitors and I made my way to the main entrance.

The sky was now more or less uncluttered apart from a few flamingo-pink streaks crisscrossing on the horizon to the west. I walked under an arch made by two rows of American elms to what was originally a Colonial mansion. The entrance had been added on sometime in the 1930s. Pastel-paint concrete and glass doors.

I made my way to the reception desk where a plump middle-aged woman with her dark hair tied in a bun was staring at a computer screen. I took off my hat.

"I'm looking for Rabbi Rifkin," I said.

She responded without looking up.

"Are you a visitor?"

A star of David as big as a doughnut hung on a gold chain over the top of her white uniform. The name engraved on the badge was Bettina de Vries.

"I called earlier," I told her. "My name is Harry Lipkin. I believe Rabbi Rifkin is a patient here."

Bettina de Vries entered the information on her computer and waited. Then she read out what was on the screen.

"His room is 106, in the Sherman Wing," she said. "But he usually spends this time of day in the garden. You get there through the main corridor. Make a left by the catering area and then a right. You'll find him easy enough. He sits by the aviary."

Bettina de Vries handed me a plastic visitor's card and a ball point with the name of the medical center embossed on the side. She had used her left hand. I looked for a wedding ring. There wasn't one.

"The garden is security sensitive," she said. "You will need the number printed on the back of the card to get back into the building. You just press the buttons in sequence. One. Nine. Zero. Nine. Please sign the visitor's book, print your name under the signature, provide your driver's license number, and fill in the time and date you arrived."

"I got a passport back home if you need it," I said, filling in the page. "The photo's a little out of date but you can tell it's me. I'm wearing the same tie."

Nothing to that. Bettina de Vries was busy checking through my entry.

"Hang the ID around your neck," she ordered. "If you get lost, call out. There will always be a nurse somewhere close. They will help you."

"I'll manage just fine," I said and put my hat back on. "I'm pretty good at finding my way around places I never been before. Last Sukkoth I hiked alone through the Big Cypress. Six days wandering in the swamps with nothing but a compass and a bowie knife."

Bettina de Vries's mouth did something funny. A sort of twitch like when you suffer a minor stroke. But she didn't speak.

She pressed a button under her desk. Doors opened. I gave her the Oliver Hardy Kiddy Finger Wave and shoved the ID into my pocket. A silk scarf I put around my neck. Not cheap blue ribbon with a lump of plastic hanging from the end. To hell with ID cards.

Then I shuffled off through the glass doors to look for Rabbi Rifkin.

TWENTY-TWO

Harry and Rabbi Rifkin Talk

He was in his wheelchair. Sitting by a large aviary at the far end of a wide lawn surrounded by pale lilac rhododendrons and cherry-red azaleas. His beard had grown a couple of feet since I had last seen him and there was less hair under his old black velvet yarmulke. He was wearing a heavy dressing gown and had a thick wool blanket over his lap. Two large white surgical patches covered his eyes.

"Guess who?" I said, going close.

It took a moment for the old rabbi to put a name to the voice and a face to the name.

"Harry Lipkin." A pause. "You checking in?"

I put a hand out and patted Rabbi Rifkin on the shoulder.

"Depends on the catering," I said.

He made a sound. The sound we make when something's lousy.

"That bad?" I said.

"I've eaten better. But since I am not paying, I'm not complaining."

"Makes sense."

"Sure it makes sense. Why shouldn't it?"

It could have gone on like that for some time. Rabbis and their hypothetical this and their hypothetical that. It's their job. I let it go.

There was a short silence, then Lionel Rifkin waved his hand to a place behind me.

"There are some garden chairs, Harry," he said. "Near where you came in. Pull one over here. Sit by me."

I did as I was told. "The eyes, Lionel?" I asked. He said nothing. I asked again. I knew it was an intrusion but I couldn't stop myself. "The wraps? How come?"

He laughed. "They don't ask me about Judgment Day. I don't ask them about eyesight."

A Florida scrub jay landed on a perch in the aviary close enough to throw seed at us and listened in.

"You don't have to tell me," I said. "None of my business."

"No big deal, Harry," he said. "Detached retinas."

"Both of them?"

He nodded.

"Unlucky."

Another nod. And a shrug.

"But they can fix retinas now."

"Some," the rabbi said. "My sight has gone, Harry. Gone for good."

I had known Lionel Rifkin a long time. Nothing I could think of saying would be of any comfort. He gestured to the cage.

"I spend my days out here by the aviary," he continued. "Listening to them sing, under their wire sky. Cardinals. Mockingbirds. Waxwings . . ."

He stopped talking. Listened. A bird chirped. He smiled to himself. Then he carried on.

"There's a nurse from Poland, Harry, who looks after me. Kasia. She knows about birds. She comes out here and tells me who sings what. I can already tell most of the birds here by their song. What we just heard was a pipit."

He paused. Sighed. Shifted in his chair. Adjusted his blanket. Sorrow dropped by. Hung around. Then went.

"Sometimes she holds my hand," he said.

I left it before I spoke again. Let it settle. The mood. And I looked at him. Closer. The two big white cotton wool patches. His high beaked nose. The white beard and what was left of his hair. He'd become a bird. An owl. A snowy owl. It suited him but I didn't say so. I told him instead why I was there.

"Lionel," I said. "I need some information. The kind I figure you can supply."

The rabbi moved his head. "Tell me."

"I am on a case."

"I didn't think it was for a lecture on pipits."

"I am working for a woman called Norma Weinberger," I explained. "She lives in Fort Lauderdale. Her late husband made hats."

Rabbi Rifkin threw his arms in the air. The blanket fell off his lap onto the grass.

"No kidding? Isaac Weinberger."

I picked up the blanket and put it back.

"You know him?"

"I think I buried him. He was the only Jew I ever met without a sense of humor. I once told him the story of the unknown Jewish soldier. You heard it?" He didn't wait to hear me say the entire Jewish population heard it. He made himself comfortable.

"There's a cemetery and in it is a memorial to the unknown Jewish soldier. On the stone is carved the name. Manny Rosen. Born 1923. Died 1943. A Gentile comes along and sees the memorial. He is puzzled. He notices an elderly Jew standing by. He decides to ask the Jew for an explanation. The Gentile says, can you tell me something? If I can, replies the Jew. The Gentile says if this is a memorial to the unknown soldier, how come you know his name? Simple, the Jew says. As a tailor, Manny Rosen was known. But as a soldier . . . ?"

We both went through the motions of laughing. Not as loud as the first time we heard it. But loud enough to scare the Florida scrub jay into taking cover.

The rabbi stroked his beard.

"Isaac Weinberger," he said. "A humorous bankrupt. His wife was a handsome woman, Harry. When I knew her. Real handsome."

"Still is."

"Had the look of that film star. You know the one."

"Doris Day."

"But with dark hair."

"Someone is stealing her valuables," I said. "Someone who works for her."

Rabbi Rifkin made a tutting noise.

"I'm stuck for a motive," I said. "The motive is the same for all her employees. Each one needs more than they get paid. One has to be stronger than the rest. I figured you might help."

He shrugged.

"From weddings and bar mitzvahs I know. But from motives? Anyhow. Try me, Harry. You never know."

I gave it to him.

"The guy who cooks for Mrs. Weinberger is an Ethiopian Jew. Amos Moses. He sends money home. They are rebuilding the synagogue. But there's no way I can check that. It could be just a cover. I need to know for certain that Amos is on the level."

The rabbi thought. Birds sang. A warm breeze crossed the garden. His thinking bore fruit.

"The man you want is Arlen Klein," he said. "When Beth Jacob closed as a schul and linked up with the Jewish Museum, they put Klein in to run the appeals and charity work. Call him. Tell him I told you to. If there's a man called Amos Moses sending money home, he'll know."

A bell chimed in the main building. Rabbi Rifkin tapped his stomach.

"Time to eat, Harry," the rabbi said. "You want to give me a push?"

I got up and wheeled Lionel Rifkin back silently across the lawn and all the way to the dining room. It made me feel useful in a way I hadn't felt for a long time.

I parked Rabbi Rifkin at his supper table dressed with a single lily in a slender vase and a fresh napkin rolled into a silver ring and a table card with his name printed on it.

"Thanks a lot, Lionel," I said. "You have been a big help."

The rabbi gave me a fragile smile.

"God bless you, Harry," he said.

He couldn't see it but I smiled back.

· TWENTY-THREE ·

Lieutenant Voss Returns with Some
Unexpected News

t was late when I got back home. The screen that they had erected around the dead kid was still on my front path but the cops and cadaver had gone. I made myself a glass of warm milk and ate two hazelnut and apple cookies. Then I put my dentures in water and went to bed.

I was in a deep sleep when a chime from the doorbell woke me. I checked my bedside clock. It said five after seven.

It was too early for the mailman and too late for the day laborers. People who ask if they can cut my lawn, put the tiles of my roof back, paint the front of the house, fix the plumbing, and service my Chevy. And they'll do it all for five bucks.

I put on my dressing gown and opened the door half awake.

It was Lieutenant Voss. Same crumpled shirt. Same pants that needed a press. Same sharp eyes.

"The day watch out of homicide?" I asked and coughed for five minutes.

He waited for the noise to die down.

"Six to four," he said. "But I get plenty done."

I led him through the passage and into the kitchen.

"Take a seat while I make some coffee," I said. "You want a cup?"

He nodded. Nothing else.

I put water and fresh coffee in the percolator and switched on the heat.

"You got a reason to call?" I said. "Or were you just passing and thought you'd drop by?"

"A kid dies," he said. "A kid in a smart suit. It looks like an accident. Maybe it is. Maybe it isn't. The kid has no ID. The only witness says the kid was a Christian missionary. The witness is a private investigator. He has a valid license to practice in the state of Florida. The private investigator has been around. He knows the score. His client comes first. He plays it that way. But his way doesn't suit City Hall."

He left a pause. The smell of fresh-brewed coffee filled it.

"The kid that died here," Lieutenant Voss carried on. "On your path. Yesterday around noon. Guess what we found?"

"I just got out of bed," I said. "Later I do guessing. Right now I do coffee."

I took two mugs and placed them on the kitchen table.

"When we got the kid back to the morgue," Voss said, "I looked at his Italian shoes. His imported Italian suit. His handmade ninety-dollar shirt. The dead kid's outfit would cost me a year's salary. It didn't add up. Selling God door to door. You'd get your pants and jacket from Kmart. Not Armani."

"Maybe his old man mined diamonds," I said. "All kinds of people get wrapped up in religion."

I handed Voss his coffee.

"We took his prints," he said. "As a matter of routine."

I took a sip of coffee. It was hot. But I went cold. The prints. Harry. Schmuck. You forgot the prints.

"The kid we took to the morgue sold narcotics," Voss said. "His name was Redlan Donny Collins. Nineteen years old. His pals called him Little Chill. He spent his brief time on Earth dealing dope in every state with a coastline from here to New Jersey."

I looked at Voss.

"So the kid sold narcotics. What's that to me?"

"If you are mixed up in something I want to know," he said.

I thought about it. Then I gave him a little.

"Okay, Voss," I said. "Cop to cop. The kid sold dope

to someone who works for a client of mine. He came to lean on me."

Voss drained his mug.

"Nice coffee," he said.

He undid the front button of his jacket and made himself comfortable.

"You got a name for me, Harry?"

"You got a reason to know?"

He gave me that washed-out look cops develop over the years.

"Do I have to remind you that it is a criminal offense to use narcotics as well as to sell them? And that to be an accessory to a crime is also criminal?"

He was fishing in a shallow stream and hoping something would bite.

"The tile killed the kid, Voss," I said. "That is all you are getting. All you need. Fill in your report and put 'no suspicious circumstances' at the bottom. Then take the rest of the day off."

Lieutenant Voss didn't like it. I was holding something back. He knew. But he let it go. I had a hunch there was something else on his mind.

"If that's the way you want it," he said.

I said nothing.

Voss took a card from his inside jacket pocket and placed it on the table next to his mug.

"But if you think of something you think I should know, my number's here. Call me. Day or night."

I picked up the card and put it in my dressing gown pocket. The policeman drank from his coffee.

"Something else," he said. "Something you might have missed."

I waited.

"If you had killed Redlan Collins, Harry, you would be two hundred grand better off."

It wasn't what I had expected.

"How's that?" I asked. "Did he mention me in his will?"

Voss moved to the door.

"That's the price on the wanted posters. The money the state put up to see our recently dear departed 'Little Chill' in a denim suit with stripes. Tell your tale another way, Mr. Lipkin, and you could be a rich man."

Voss gave me time to think it through.

"And you would make it official?" I asked.

"Sure," he said. "I would say that you told me the kid pulled a gun and you hit him with a tile. Self-defense. Open and shut. They might even give you a medal as well as the bounty."

"You'd fix it like that?"

"For ten percent," he said. "Think it over."

"I thought it over," I said. "It stinks. Collins was killed by an act of God. Nothing else. Lean on Jehovah for your ten percent, Voss, and don't come bothering me again."

"And I thought you were bright," he said.

"Bright enough to tell your captain you were looking to pervert the course of justice," I told him tough as it needed. "For a cut of the reward."

I looked him over. A police officer nearing the end of his time. His pension would scarcely fill his billfold. There'd be nothing left over after a week. Nothing extra to put aside. No badge. No free bullets. Every day the same. Lots of time to fill. All day every day. But it was a schnorrer's trick to try to deal himself in. And his messing with my case would slow me down. He was best off my back.

The lieutenant stared at me. Hard. A long time. His eyes didn't blink once. Then he turned and walked out the room. I figured I'd seen the last of Voss.

· TWENTY-FOUR ·

Harry Gets Busy at Home

Once Voss was out of the house I went into my office and called the Beth Jacob. I told Arlen Klein the reason for my call. He said he was busy but offered an hour for lunch.

It was still early. I had plenty of time to take a long shower and get ready before driving over to the Beth Jacob.

The bathroom overlooked my neighbor's patio. I could hear them talking. At least I could hear Mrs. Feldman talking. In the years I had been living next to the Feldmans I had never heard Morton Feldman say more than a couple of sentences. Mrs. Feldman did his talking for him. Today she was talking for ten Morton Feldmans.

"Are you listening to me, Morton? Those white sheet things they put up. In his front yard. And the police there all day. The man with the camera taking photos.

The ambulance. *Feh.* Don't argue with me, Morton. I am telling you. He killed someone. I know it. That Harry Lipkin. *Tsuris.* What have I said all along? A man they should lock up. *Gloib mir.* For his own good."

I picked a dry towel from the hook behind the bathroom door and spent the next half hour it takes me these days to dry off. Then I hung my towel back on the hook and went into my bedroom and got myself dressed. I turned on the clock radio and tuned into a local jazz station. I put on my pants to Woody Herman's "Woodchopper's Ball." And I put a knot in my bow tie to Earl Hines's "My Monday Date."

The bow tie was from Savile Row. Red silk with small black polka dots. My cousin Leon brought it back from a trip he made. Two days in London. Two days in Paris. Two days in Dublin. Two weeks in bed recovering.

Dressed for the day I went to the office to see if anyone had called while I was in the shower. Some people can hear the phone ring under water. Not me. The red light was blinking on the machine and a little number told me that I had one call. I pressed the button and played it back.

"Hi, Harry. How you doing? It's Oscar Letto. I asked around for you. About the butler. Mr. Lee. He has a reputation. Lucky Lee. That's what they call him around here. Like you say. He only comes one day a week. Never

more. And he never bets on anything over evens. On a six-month run my information is Lee could be looking at anything between ten and twenty grand. That kind of money buys a lot of steamed rice. If he needed to steal from your client to make extra he'd need to do a lot better from it than he does at Gulfstream. Let me know if I can help you further."

I pressed the button and the machine went back to recording mode. No sooner had the red light come back on than the phone rang again. I picked up the receiver. Mrs. Weinberger didn't even give me a chance to say "Harry Lipkin. Private Investigator. How can I help?" She was straight in. No hello? No how are you? No is this a bad moment? Bang. In.

"*A Klog iz mir.* That no-good gonif has struck again. During the night. And you will have no idea what he stole. They broke into my desk and stole a bundle of love letters tied with ribbon that my dear Isaac wrote me. Letters he wrote when we first met. I had taken them to read before I went to bed, as I sometimes do. Reading them makes me both happy and sad at the same time, mostly sad. I put them back in the drawer in my desk and this morning when I was looking in the drawer for something else they were gone. I looked through the drawer I don't know how many times. My love letters. Stolen while I slept."

I tried to imagine a love letter written by Isaac Weinberger. There wasn't time. And his widow was still talking.

"How do you explain it, Mr. Lipkin? Who would do such a thing?"

"That's what you are paying me to find out," I said.

There was a short edgy pause. When she spoke again her voice was more nervous than scared.

"Would you do something extra for me, Mr. Lipkin? A little more than maybe I have the right to ask?"

"Try me," I said. "As long as it's not fixing roof tiles. Nothing that needs a ladder."

She let it go.

"I just want you to spend the night here. At my home. It came to me suddenly. While I was taking my early morning dip. If you were here. You might catch the thief red-handed."

It wasn't a bad idea. Something I could never have suggested. Not even if I had thought of it myself. A night in a client's house. A widow sleeping alone. Me hiding in a dark corner with nothing to do from lights out to reveille. Better it came from her.

"When did you have in mind?" I said.

"I'll leave it to you, Mr. Lipkin."

"In a couple of days," I suggested. "There's some work to do before I pack my denture cream and dressing gown."

There was a gap.

"A lot of men would take my request a different way," she said. "You know what I mean?"

"Don't give it another thought," I said.

She sighed. "If only there were more men like you."

"If there were," I said, "I'd be out of a job."

Norma Weinberger hung up and I wrote in my notebook to check in at Coral Gables soon as I had time.

On the drive to the Beth Jacob I got to thinking over the information Oscar Letto had left me. Lucky Lee was fast joining Steve in putting himself pretty well in the clear.

Harry Drives to Miami Beach

crossed Biscayne Bay and took the J. F. Kennedy Causeway through North Bay Island, North Bay Village, and Treasure Island to Miami Beach. I made a right onto Collins Avenue where grass grows in scruffy patches out of the dirty pale gold sand on one side and rows of tall tufted-head palms grow on the other. Behind the trees are the hotels. Six miles of them. Same size. Same price. Same everything. The only difference is the name over the entrance. The Beach Hotel. Hotel Beach. They built Miami to come to. From New York when it snows or Oklahoma when they got done barn dancing and cutting corn as high as an elephant's eye. And they built it big enough and smart enough for visitors to want to come back.

Tourists. A species Darwin missed.

Twelve million people with a suitcase on wheels and nothing that's as good as they get back home. And that's just the Jews. They sit on benches writing a postcard home. I could write it for them. We are having a swell time and the weather is great and it only rained the day we arrived and the room overlooks the beach and tomorrow we will be doing the Everglades and the day after Orlando to meet a college kid dressed up as Mickey Mouse.

If I was in the postcard business I'd get a picture of Miami Beach and print the message on the back. All you would have to do is sign your name and stick on a stamp.

Every now and then during the tourist season you'd see someone who was born in Miami. Someone who actually lives there. All year round. Pays city taxes. You'd know them right off. They would be my age and look like somebody who would rather be living someplace else.

I crawled by Loews Hotel and thought about the time when it was just an Art Deco joint called the St. Moritz. Hannah Levinsky had her wedding reception there. 1939. Seventy years before it became the most expensive hotel redevelopment ever on Miami Beach.

Hannah Levinsky. Eyes the color of topaz and rose pink lips that tasted of honey. We had fun together. Hannah and me. That was before she married Roy Burman and his father's fur business. At the time Hannah got married Burman's old man had the third biggest tiled bathroom in Florida.

Drivers parking caused a crawl. People with walkers were moving faster.

During the stop–start–slow down I thought some more about Maria. Polite. Honest. Noble. More than pretty. Hardworking Maria Lopez had kind of slipped from my mind a little. All she had was a maid's salary to send dough back to her father and help pay for her brother's bail. Maria worked six days a week. I tried to think of a job that she could do one day a week and maybe nights to earn the kind of money she needed. I couldn't think of one. Not a legal one anyway.

The traffic picked up and I swung right onto Fourth Street and left onto Washington Avenue. I would take another look at Maria. As soon as I had got through checking Amos Moses's story with Arlen Klein.

· TWENTY-SIX ·

Harry Meets Arlen Klein

Outside Beth Jacob was a palm tree growing out of a tub that someone had decorated with fairy lights and a sign that said Keep Smiling. I parked next to it and crossed the street.

The man who I guessed was Arlen Klein was standing on the bottom step of Beth Jacob. He was holding a bulky leather briefcase and looking at his wristwatch. He wore a Homburg hat, a *beketshe* and white shirt unbuttoned at the neck. He was wider than he was tall.

"Arlen Klein?" I asked.

The silent reply came with a nod you'd miss if you blinked.

"I am Harry Lipkin. The private eye who called earlier."

He lifted his watch to his eyes and stared at its face through the inch-thick lenses of his spectacles. They were the kind they prescribe for people with myopia. There was a kid at school who had spectacles with those lenses. He got teased bad. You took off his spectacles and he couldn't move without bumping into things. We laughed at him. The way kids laugh at deformity. He became a nuclear scientist. Won the Nobel Prize.

"You're late," Arlen Klein said as blunt as a butter knife. "And I am a very busy man."

"There was an accident," I said. "And heavy traffic."

He wasn't interested.

"I get no help," he said. "I got Rabbi Saltzmann. Some help. I give him a job to do and it takes him a week. A simple job. Send this letter. Make a call. The museum gave him a computer. From new. He sold it to his son-in-law for fifty dollars. I get an hour to eat. Now I got forty-five minutes."

Klein moved off and I tagged behind.

He had little legs. Little legs that moved extra fast under a hungry body. I struggled to keep him in view.

"There's a deli a couple blocks down from here," he called back to me. "Kosher. Saul's. Saul does lunch for a dollar twenty. Keep up, Mr. Lipkin. Walk fast. They get full early."

Saul's was two blocks south of Beth Jacob. There was already a line waiting for takeout but a few tables were still free. The waiter found us a place under a canopy on the sidewalk. I got my breath back and we ordered. Pastrami on rye for Klein. Chicken liver and potato salad for me. Lemon tea for two.

The waiter wrote it down and drifted off.

Klein took off his spectacles and rubbed his eyes. He put his spectacles back on and did his best to look at me.

"I understand that you want some information about contributions to Ethiopia?" Klein asked.

"Rabbi Rifkin figured you would know."

"Rabbi Rifkin was right," he said. "If I don't know about contributions to Ethiopia, no one knows about contributions to Ethiopia. You can take it from me. When it comes to Ethiopian contributions made in this part of the world, there is no one who knows more."

He let me take it in. If he could have reached he would have given himself a pat on the back.

"Anything on paper I could look through?" I said.

Klein opened his briefcase and handed me a single sheet of paper full of figures.

"These are all the contributions sent to me in the last month," he said. "I keep a monthly account. The figures you have in your hand are typical of the last three years. I have accounts going all the way back to when we began collecting aid."

"Impressive," I said.

Klein jabbed a finger to roughly where I was reading.

"The left-hand column shows the donors. As you can see. Amos Moses sends donations once a month. They are listed in the right-hand column. Every dollar. Every cent. You can see for yourself."

The order arrived. Klein ate while I scanned the numbers.

"Amos is doing a fine job," I said and handed back the sheet of paper.

Klein put it away and wiped his mouth with a napkin.

"The world needs a lot more like Amos Moses," he said and stuck his arm in the air for the waiter to see.

The waiter gestured he'd be right over.

"Take it from me, Mr. Lipkin," Klein said. "If you are looking for a rotten apple, take my advice. Look someplace else."

Arlen Klein grabbed his briefcase.

"Got to go," he said. "Give my best regards to Rabbi Rifkin."

Klein said nothing more. He squeezed his way into the street and sprinted back the way we came. There was a lot to think over and three dollars forty to pay.

Lee. Steve. And now Amos. Someone should make it into a movie. *Crime Without Motive.* They could write me a walk-on part as the dumb dick.

I left five bucks on the plate and walked back to my car.

· TWENTY-SEVEN ·

Harry Makes Some Calls

On my way back to Warmheart I thought more about Rufus and Maria. The two suspects I had not checked out.

The maid's story sounded on the level but the sums didn't add up. Bail and medicine bite deep into anyone's salary. Forget making beds and polishing brass six days a week. That pays for nothing. An aspirin and a day out of jail at most.

Rufus looked the part. But all I had was hearsay.

I decided to take a closer look at both of them. And I would do it without them knowing. A tail was the only way. Putting one on Maria would need careful planning. Maids work shifts. Shifts get changed. For all kinds of petty reasons.

But Rufus Davenport was an easy ride. All I had to do was buy a ticket and watch him fight. He said he was good. It wouldn't take me long to find out. Ten seconds of round one.

Back in my office I called Eddie Berkowitz at the gym. Before he passed away my friend Abe Schultz got me a phone you can walk around the house with. No cord. Abe didn't do too much toward the end of his life. He didn't do too much in the beginning. Or in the middle. Abe was just a nice guy. Good-hearted and well meaning. If he had a job it was to be around. A baseball game. A day at the track. You called Abe and he'd come. Wherever he was.

The place got better when Abe was there.

While I waited for someone to answer at Eddie's end, I took my phone to the window.

Some people watch passing clouds to kill time. Or butterflies. I watch the Feldmans. They were heading off for an early bird supper. It was the evening they went to Mario's Pasta and Pizza Hut. Not Gino's Piazza and Pasta House. Mario's. The pizzas were better. A lot better. I heard Mrs. Feldman tell her husband. More than once.

I also ate at Mario's when my dentures felt up to it. His pizzas were only so-so but I liked him. After six vodkas I liked him a lot.

Mario was born in the Ukraine. His real name was Igor. Before he came to the USA Igor had never eaten a pizza. He'd never even heard of pizza. And he sure as hell never cooked one. But it didn't bother him. To Mario a

BARRY FANTONI

pizza was a flat lump of dough with burned edges that just about fits on the plate and is covered with tomato sauce and hot sausage and melted cheese you can't chew or cut, and if you didn't want to eat it sitting down in his place he'd pop it in a cardboard box with his name printed on the top and you could heat it up when you got home and eat it sitting in front of the TV. A pizza. It's a pizza. Nothing to it. Everyone except an Italian would agree with him.

The Feldmans were in line at the free bus stop along with two dozen other starving Jews who hadn't eaten anything since lunch. Apart from the two slices of apple cake and maybe a little fruit salad.

Warmheart ran its own free bus service for citizens over sixty. So that meant everyone. Muriel Feldman had the arrival and departure times etched deeper into her head than the ink on a treasury bill. It arrived outside their place. Once a day. Five days a week. At four twenty-eight on the nail.

"Nothing to pay, today," Imran, the driver, would grin when they climbed aboard. "Free bus. Free country."

Imran from Iran. His father was a professor of mathematics. Imran once told me that his father had said in public that girls should be educated same as boys. The police threw him in jail. Seven years ago. One day Imran and his pals would change all that. Call Iran by the old name. The name they used when Persians created build-

· 138 ·

ings and music and art and literature and sciences you couldn't put a price on. Some place. Persia. Then.

Finally someone answered the phone at Eddie's end. The man who answered wasn't Eddie.

"Yeah?" the voice said.

"I'm a friend of Eddie," I said.

"And?"

"There's a boxer called Frank Dunlop."

"And?"

"I need to know when he is next fighting?"

"You gotta name, bud?"

"Lipkin."

"Hold the line."

I looked at the minute hand on my wall clock. It moved five times before the voice came back.

"I got a list here. Eddie left it on his desk. In case someone by the name of Lipkin called."

"Eddie's not there?" I said.

"It's his grandson's birthday. Eight years old."

"Kids."

"Kids."

"And Dunlop?"

"Fighting tonight."

"Do you have an address?"

"I got a list."

"Does the list say where?"

"He's on the undercard. Second fight."

"And where is it? The second fight?"

"Same place as the first."

"And that is where?"

"Naples."

"Do you have the name of the venue?"

"The White House Hotel."

"And the time?"

"Eight on the dot."

I made a note. "Thanks."

"Sure."

"Say hello to Eddie."

"Sure."

"Tell him I hope he had a nice day with his grandson."

"Sure."

We hung up. I took another look at the minute hand on my clock. If I set off right away I would easy make Naples by the time Frank Dunlop climbed through the ropes.

· TWENTY-EIGHT ·

*Harry Sees Rufus Davenport aka
Frank Dunlop in Action*

The White House Hotel was one of thousands strung out alongside Highway 41. They began in southern Florida and fizzled out in Michigan. When they built Highway 41 I was in short pants. The White House Hotel was nothing but a vacant lot covered in grass stubble. Rusted junk and palm trees. Now it was a thirty-four-story glass tower with three pools, five hundred rooms, six restaurants, nine conference rooms, twenty tennis courts, a health spa, golf course, helicopter pad, a parking lot the size of Tasmania, and staff that spoke every language but American.

I parked and bought a ticket to the Henry Kissinger Conference Room, where they were staging the fights.

The ring was set up in the center of around fifty tables covered in white linen and dinner plates and silver baskets full of bread rolls. In the ring the local bantamweight with bloody cuts above two shut eyes and a busted mouth heard that he had won by a majority decision.

A tall blond waitress with a lot of leg on show wandered over and asked if I wanted a drink. I ordered a blended Scotch neat and made myself comfortable. I didn't want a blended Scotch. A lemon tea would have been a whole lot more welcome. But lemon tea at the ringside? It's like the Fastest Gun in the West asking the barman for milk.

"Blended Scotch neat coming up," the waitress said without a smile and headed toward the bar.

I sat on a chair near a table where a group of a hundred and fifty Japanese were taking photos. Yoshi smiling. Hiroki smiling. Kaito smiling. One day the world will end. The Eiffel Tower will go. The Leaning Tower of Pisa. The Statue of Liberty and the Taj Mahal. Gone. All of it. The wonders of the world from Ayers Rock to Elvis Presley's grave. Dust. Everything. Well. Almost everything. Someplace there'd be a Japanese tourist smiling.

My drink arrived. I needed it. The long drive had left me beat. I wasn't looking for a long night as well as the long drive home.

I sipped the liquor and watched the emcee introduce the next two contestants. He read the names from a scrap of paper.

"In the blue corner," he crooned into his mic. "Frank 'The Fist' Dunlop. And in the red corner. Mike 'Killer' Bollinger."

No one cheered. No one clapped. No one noticed.

The bell went. And that was it. The first punch Rufus landed was an upper cut. Right hand. It was thrown from just below his chest and traveled six inches. The glove carrying 234 pounds ripped through Bollinger's thin defenses and smacked him full on his chin. He dropped. Faceup. Eyes wide open staring at nothing. Jaw slack. Gum shield gone. Body limp. Not even a twitch. The referee counted ten with the fingers of both hands and waved the bout over.

There was no mistake. The boxer I had just seen working was everything he said he was. I did some simple accountancy. The standard purse for an undercard out-of-town fight is two hundred and fifty bucks. The manager takes fifty. That leaves two hundred to take home to the wife and kids. Sure. Two hundred bucks is not the same as two grand. But boxing is legal and stealing jade isn't.

I took out my notebook and scratched Rufus Davenport, also known as Frank Dunlop, off the list.

I looked at my watch. It was just after nine.

I thought about dropping by Norma Weinberger's for a little late-night snooping but my eyes were growing sleepy and the bits of me with arthritis were waking up. Finger joints. Toes. Hips. Elbow. Back. Top and lower. My painkillers were in the bathroom cabinet.

I paid the tab and drove home.

· TWENTY-NINE ·

Harry Plans to Tail Maria

I put the Chevy in the garage and my hat on the hook. I hung my jacket under my hat. I changed my brogues for my house shoes and undid my tie. Then I went to the kitchen and made a glass of lemon tea and carried it through to the sofa. After a couple of sips I realized I was too tired to drink it all. I went back to the kitchen and emptied what I hadn't drunk into the sink and washed the glass and placed the washed glass on the stainless-steel draining board alongside the pile of clean pans and pots and cutlery and cups and saucers and all the other stuff I use to cook and eat. I then put the house to sleep and went to bed.

The night was cooler than usual but it wasn't the slight chill that kept me awake. It was Maria. A maid without a passport gets paid a free bed and food. It's the standard salary when you work illegally. A maid with signed papers picks up a couple of hundred bucks a month. Maximum. There was only one answer. She had to have a second salary. A job she did in her free time. Florida offered a choice. Fast-food joints. All-night drugstores. Gas stations.

In the morning I would find out.

I woke just after seven, got myself some breakfast, showered, dressed, and by ten I was ready to call Coral Gables and speak to Mr. Lee. He'd know Maria's moves. It was his job to organize them.

"Harry Lipkin," I said.

"Good morning, sir. I trust you are well."

"Swell. You?"

"As well as one should expect." He paused. "And is sir wishing to speak with Mrs. Weinberger?"

"To get Maria's work schedule," I told him. "I need it. The nights she works. The days she works. The nights she goes out. The nights she stays home."

"If sir would care to hold the line," he said, "I shall check."

I got to figure Mr. Lee. This way. He was the kind of guy who could bite into a double cream cheese bagel with lox, chicken liver, pickled herring, mayo, ketchup, and mustard and not drop any over his pants. You didn't meet them often. Until I met Mr. Lee I hadn't met one.

Mr. Clean Pants came back on the line. "Is sir there?"

"Pencil at the ready."

"Will sir be making a note?"

A figure of speech, Mr. Lee. "I am listening."

The butler cleared his throat.

"Mrs. Weinberger's maid normally remains on duty until Mrs. Weinberger retires. This is usually between seven and seven-thirty. The exceptions are those evenings when bridge is played or during a period of religious observance."

I started to count them out in my head.

"There's at least one a month," I said. "Yom Kippur. Hanukkah. Passover. Rosh Hashanah. Sukkoth . . . Sometimes more."

Mr. Lee agreed. "Sir is correct. Twenty, to the best of my knowledge."

"And Maria works every one?"

"That is how it stands. Yes, sir."

"And Friday? The day of rest?"

"Miss Lopez has Friday afternoons to herself and a free weekend every three months."

I added it up. A couple of hours at night and a few days. If Maria worked for someone else as well as Mrs. Weinberger it had to be the best paid part-time job in town.

"Tell me, Mr. Lee," I asked, "does Maria stick around after she's through work? Read a book in her room? Watch TV?"

"I have the distinct impression, sir," he said, "that Miss Lopez goes out of the house."

"Have you any idea where she might go?"

He'd talked enough. He had other duties. Nothing to do with me.

"Alas not, sir," he said through a half-masked yawn. "What Miss Lopez does in her free time, sir, I consider none of my business."

"But it is mine," I snapped. "I am being paid to find a thief and you are going to help. Like it or not."

He didn't like it. But I was holding the ace. Me boss. Him slave.

"What is it that sir wishes to know?"

I made it simple. "When is Maria Lopez off next?"

He made it short. "It is this evening, I believe, sir."

"Wasn't so tough, was it?" I said.

There was a pause.

"Will that be all?"

"Tell Mrs. Weinberger I called," I said. "Tell her not to worry. Tell her the case is taking shape. There's a chink of light."

I hung up and went through it once more. If Maria could make the tab working part-time it would take her off my list. But picking up a dollar-fifty a night for shoveling french fries while working for a woman with gold and diamonds worth millions. That would keep her on it. By midnight I'd know.

· THIRTY ·

Harry Tails Maria

I gave myself plenty of time. A good half hour before Maria hung up her apron I eased the Chevy off the main highway and parked on a sandy shoulder between two squat palms. From my spot I had a clear view of Coral Gables at the top of the incline. I would be able to keep track of Maria as she made her way from the servants' quarters, walked the terra-cotta path, opened the iron gates, took the slip road to the main road, headed down the hill, and hit the junction a couple of hundred yards from me in my parked car. And that is exactly what Maria Lopez did.

At just after seven-thirty Mrs. Weinberger's maid arrived at the junction. But it wasn't the Maria Lopez I knew. Not one bit.

Maria's skirt was very short. Mini and more. And it was cut from shiny leather. She had on knee-high black lace-up suede boots. The heels were six inches. Maybe more. She'd put on flame-red fishnet stockings and plenty of gold accessories and slung a white fox fur stole over what I guessed would be naked shoulders. And there were sunglasses with frames that covered half her face. A blond wig covered the rest. Whatever Mrs. Weinberger's maid did on her time off she wasn't dressed for pumping gas or grilling burgers. And she was the only person in sight.

But not for long.

A silver open-top coupe heading north accelerated past a line of five family sedans and a pickup truck and pulled up sharply across the highway from where Maria Lopez was standing. With the engine running the driver lit a cigarette and flicked the dead match into the air. He took a long pull and left the stick in his mouth. He was in a T-shirt and a fruit salad print bandana. He was around twenty. Younger even. With lightly tanned skin and the kind of cheekbones and eyes you see a lot on faces in places like Bolivia. He waited for a gap in the traffic, then he made a fast U-turn and pulled up a few feet from Maria.

Without getting out the driver opened the passenger door and Maria climbed in. She kissed the young driver on the cheek. I say a kiss but it was more a peck than a kiss. Sort of sister to brother. That kind of kiss. He didn't look at her. She didn't look at him. He did something to the dash and music came out. Loud music. A lot of drums. Trumpets. Hundreds of trumpets. Men singing falsetto Spanish. You have to develop a taste for that kind of music. It comes with developing a taste for food that comes in cold damp pancakes and sauces that can eat into lead.

The driver checked his rearview mirror, nodding his head in time to the tinny rock tumble beat, then swung the coupe back onto the highway to Miami.

A Mercedes-Benz SLR McLaren Roadster is not an easy automobile to tail. Driven fast there isn't a car outside a racetrack that gets close. Driven slow you might glimpse smoke from the exhaust in the distance. But the driver kept to the rules. Nothing flash. Fifty-five steady. As if he didn't want to attract any attention to himself. Or his passenger.

He used U.S. Route 1. No turns or deviations. It was early evening traffic. Mostly people heading into Miami for the night. There was plenty to do. You could fall asleep during a concert of popular classics on the beach. Wonder why you had paid fifty bucks for an Elvis Memorial Concert or sit in an empty theater and watch another new play about AIDS.

I tailed the couple without having to use too much of my arthritic toe on the gas. I didn't lose sight of its out-of-state license once. Since Maria had never seen my car I knew I could tag along unnoticed.

It was dark when we drove into downtown Miami and road signs for Miami International Airport mixed in with all the others. When the Dixie Highway became Brickell Avenue at SE Fourteenth Street the Mercedes edged out from the line of what was now quite slow-moving traffic and parked across from the first of a trio of five-star hotels. The car stopped outside the Atlantic Florida. Keeping my distance, I did the same.

There was a small parking lot behind some small buildings and trees across from the hotel. The Mercedes backed into the entrance and Maria got out. She and the driver spoke a few words and then the driver inched back onto Brickell Avenue and headed on south. I parked in the lot and followed Maria.

Keeping close to her wasn't tough. Maria Lopez's high heels reduced her speed to fifty feet an hour. The hundred and twenty-nine yards to the hotel took five minutes and thirty-two seconds. Give or take.

THIRTY-ONE

Harry Discovers Maria's Secret

The Atlantic Florida's lobby is softly lit satinwood walls and peach mirrors and dark leather seats. And lots of plants in square tubs. Even an out-of-season standard room cost six hundred a week. In season a penthouse suite cost three hundred a night. The view was the same. Biscayne Bay and a row of cheaper hotels on the other side.

The place was busy but not noisy. A party of Canadians was checking in. Thirty guys in baseball caps with maple leafs on the front and bags full of fishing gear. You could tell. Three sold automobiles. Two sold fur boots and the rest sold real estate. There weren't any Mounties.

Maria edged round them and made her way to the elevator. I followed, keeping my distance before moving to a spot by a wall outside Maria's range of vision. The elevator emptied. Maria waited. Checked that she was alone and then got on board. I watched the numbers over the elevator door. They didn't light until the elevator reached the penthouse. It didn't have a number. Just the letter *P*.

The main lobby led into a lounge. I found a seat across from the elevator and made myself comfortable. After a short while a waiter stopped by. The name pinned to a badge on his well-pressed vest was Jerry.

"Can I bring you something, sir?" he asked.

I took the notebook out of my pocket and wrote down the license plate number of the Mercedes I'd tailed. Under it I added a phone number. I tore the page out and gave it to him.

"Call the bottom number," I said. "And ask the guy on the other end to find out what car the top number belongs on. The guy you'll be talking to is Victor Morrow. Tell him you are doing it for Harry Lipkin."

Jerry looked at the piece of paper. Then at me. "Is this legal, sir?"

He paused for my reaction. There wasn't one.

"You understand, I have to ask?" he said.

I handed Jerry a ten dollar bill.

"The guy is a cop, Jerry," I explained. "He works in records and does this kind of thing privately from time to time. For old pals. Vic and me are old pals."

Jerry put the bill with the page from my notebook.

"And when I have an answer, sir?" he said.

"Bring it along with a large strong java and something nice and sweet to eat. My sugar levels need a boost and my eyelids need something to stop them closing."

Jerry was gone ten minutes. When he came back he brought the coffee, a slice of cheesecake with whipped cream, and news that the license plate and the car didn't match. The plate belonged to a four-year-old Chrysler registered in Texas.

"Was the information of use, sir?" Jerry asked.

"Real helpful."

Jerry smiled.

"I like to be of service," he said and tugged the tips of his bow tie. "It makes a job worth doing and this is a swell hotel to work in. The last place I worked they only gave you one meal a day free and you had to pay to have your uniform washed."

None of it mattered to me as much as it did to Jerry. But the phony license plate on the Mercedes mattered.

"You can do one more thing," I said. "I got to keep an eye fixed on the elevator. There's someone I am keeping tabs on who is spending the night here. If you see me snoring do something about it."

"Will a nudge be enough?"

"A nudge will do fine."

As it turned out Jerry's nudge wasn't needed. The mix of caffeine and adrenaline was plenty.

Just after four Maria stepped out of the elevator. She

hadn't bothered with the wig or the sunglasses. If she was wearing makeup I couldn't see any. She crossed the lobby like she was sleepwalking and I got up and followed her into a chilly dim Miami predawn.

The Mercedes was parked where it had been the night before. The same driver was behind the wheel. Same bandana. Same T-shirt. Same license plate. Maria let herself in and the stolen auto went back the way it came.

THIRTY-TWO

Harry Thinks It All Over

It was too late to go to bed and too early to get up. I was tired. I was aching in my back. Upper and lower. And the bit in the middle. Sharp pains wandered around the joints of my toes and fingers. Cramp was on its way. And what nature wasn't doing to me I was doing to myself. The black coffee I ordered to keep me awake was still talking with my stomach acid. And worse. Worse than all of it. I was sad. The kind of sad there is no pill for. No cure for. The sad of seeing a young and beautiful life about to get wasted. I've seen a lot of it. Bad marriages. Bad debts. Lives that had run out of time. Maria was the latest of a long line.

I took a pill for reflux and a hot shower to calm down the muscles and a deep breath to empty out the bad air in my lungs. And I thought about Little Amy.

Little Amy was the daughter of Joe and Maureen Kelly. Joe was a musician. Maureen worked in a store. Every night Joe went to work he'd walk with Little Amy to the end of the block. He'd tell her stories on the way. Then he'd kiss her and tell her to have sweet dreams. Little Amy would wave and her father would wave back while crossing the street to the subway. One night Joe waved back and didn't see the truck. Little Amy saw it all.

Without Joe's salary Maureen had to work nights. She got a job in a bar. The money was good. Drunks were generous. Tips. Offers. Maureen drank more than was good for her and one day liquor killed her.

Little Amy was completely alone. No brothers. No sisters. No one. The authorities placed her in an orphanage. After a month eating cold soup and sleeping in cold rooms Little Amy packed her bag. She had large dreamy cornflower blue eyes and soft red lips. Her hair was sunlit gold and full of wild waves that broke carelessly over her pale white shoulders.

Looking for a job. Little Amy. Fourteen. Taken for twenty. Got up in high heels and silk stockings and with an instinct where to go looking. It didn't take Little Amy long.

Her first job was to marry a retired Wall Street big shot. When not playing golf Henry Gaddis Jr. used his retirement to buy Little Amy fur coats from Bergdorf Goodman and trinkets from Tiffany. When Gaddis died Little Amy spent the six million he left her in under a year.

After the money ran out Little Amy moved to Boston and married a ninety-three-year-old widower who manufactured candy and pet food. He died. Little Amy was the sole beneficiary. Another year of throwing money around. Then she married another widower. Bradley B. Pinkerton. A long-retired something or another. Dead in a month. From what the coroner put down as natural causes. His will left her more champagne and mink.

The last of Little Amy's widowers lived here. In the State of Florida. On Ocean Ridge. He designed yachts for playboys before he'd had enough of work. It was Frank Harris who called me.

He was a man the age I am now. Worried about some medicine he'd found hidden in a cabinet that was lethal if taken in large doses. It had not been prescribed. For him or for his wife. And you wouldn't know if you'd taken it. Nor would anyone else. Not unless they cut you open and put your liver under a microscope.

But that wasn't all of it. Little Amy had made a habit of spending weekends away from home. She told him it was to see an aunt who lived alone someplace. From time to time the name of the place changed slightly. When he questioned Little Amy about the different destinations she laughed it off. Blamed Frank's hearing. Frank was worried. I told Frank I would get him some answers. It took no time. I got in my car and followed Little Orphan Amy just liked I followed Maria.

The aunt was a rock-and-roll singer with an isolated beach house on Key Largo. I gave it to Frank Harris the kindest way I knew. I told him the truth. Plain. No frills. No sentiment. When he asked where they met I gave him that too.

The last time I saw Little Amy she was still out at Key Largo. She was on her back naked on a bed. There was a single bullet hole in her breast. Her lover was beside her. He'd taken three. Chest. Throat and temple. Frank was facedown in the pool. Blood was flowing out the side of his head.

To fill time while I waited for the cops to come and tidy up I went through Little Amy's purse. It's another of those habits private eyes pick up. All part of the job of making the lines and colors of a map into a place you can walk about in. Among the loose change, perfume, credit cards, sticks of lipstick, cell phone, house keys, car keys, and a crumpled Kleenex, I found a small scuff-edged black-and-white photo of a young man. It was stuffed in a side pocket along with her compact and hand mirror. He had on a band jacket and was playing a trumpet.

Then I stopped thinking about Little Amy and started working on the case Mrs. Weinberger was paying me to solve. I wound a sheet of blank paper into the Remington and typed out what I had.

Suspect: Rufus Davenport. also known as Frank Dunlop
Occupation: Chauffeur
Other Related Interests: Boxing
Motive: A large family to support
Conclusion: A big right hook to take care of the extras
Proviso: I had only seen him fight once

Suspect: Mr. Lee
Occupation: Butler
Other Related Interests: Gambling
Motive: Gambling debts
Conclusion: No gambling debts
Proviso: Lucky Lee might not be so lucky someplace other
*   than Gulfstream*

Suspect: Steve
Occupation: Gardener
Other Related Interests: Narcotics
Motive: Paying for drugs
Conclusion: Drugs paid him
Proviso: Capable of theft if he worked in the lounge and
*   not the garden*

Suspect: Amos
Occupation: Chef
Other Related Interests: Ethiopian history
Motive: Raising funds for a new synagogue

Conclusion: An honest Joe
Proviso: At least on the surface

Suspect: Maria Lopez
Occupation: Maid
Other Related Interests: The Atlantic Florida's penthouse
Motive: Paying for her brother's bail and her father's pills
Conclusion: No one had easier access to Mrs. Weinberger's
*   rooms*
Proviso: Maria had my prayers

I was back at the start with a sheet of paper that told me I was out of time and out of ideas. The only card I had left was a night at Mrs. Weinberger's place and the hope her gonif got to work while I was there. But I'd been in the game long enough to know the odds of that happening were slim. I needed a trap and I needed bait worth biting.

I called Mrs. Weinberger. It was time to book myself in.

· THIRTY-THREE ·

Harry Prepares Mrs. Weinberger

R ing. Pause. Pause. Ring. Pause. Click.

"Mrs. Weinberger's residence."

"Hello, Lee. It's your favorite flatfoot."

"Sir?"

"Slang for gumshoe. Put me through to Mrs. Weinberger."

"Please hold."

Click. Buzz. Click.

"Hello?"

"Mrs. Weinberger? Harry Lipkin."

"Good morning!"

"You sound surprised."

"Well . . ."

"Not too early?"

"Er . . . No. I wasn't expecting you to call, that's all."

"Not interrupting anything, am I?"

"Drying off, Mr. Lipkin. My first dip of the day."

"Alone?"

"Why? Shouldn't I be?"

"I thought Maria helped you dry off."

"She does. Later. Not my first dip. Is there a reason for you to ask?"

"I don't want anyone to hear what we are saying."

"I am always alone at this hour, as the sun rises and while the day is still fresh. I read a book about meditation once that says the first hour of the day is the most important. When the mind is empty, we can fill it with fresh thoughts."

"You want me to call back?"

"No need. I am almost dry. Have you some news, Mr. Lipkin? Is that the purpose for your call? I do hope so."

I left a pause.

"Not news, exactly. More of a carefully thought-out plan."

"Well. I suppose that's something."

"Sure is. In this game, something's always better than nothing."

I let her think it through. Then I said, "We talked about me staying over. You remember?"

"I recall it very well."

"I should like to come this evening."

"Tonight?"

"If it's possible."

"So soon?"

"Sooner the better."

"Tonight is fine."

I gave it to her firmly. "Mrs. Weinberger. Everything I say from now on must go no further. Is that understood?"

"Of course."

"We have to bait a trap, Mrs. Weinberger. You follow me?"

"I think so."

"The thief must be tempted."

"Tempted? In what way, tempted?"

"Think of a mousetrap. You put out some cheese. The mouse comes out of his hole and, before he knows it, he takes a bite and snap. Curtains."

She made a shuddering sound.

"I hate mice, Mr. Lipkin. Mice and spiders. And snakes. In New York we had mice. Isaac had to call in the pest control people it got so bad. I'd be watching television or doing something and from the corner of my eye I would see this little dark thing scurrying across the floor. Luckily we have very few here."

I sighed.

"But you do have a thief."

"I am fully aware of it. Not a minute passes without the thought of my precious belongings being taken from under my very nose."

"The strategy I have worked out will be risky."

"I am prepared."

"You will have to put on display a genuinely valuable piece of jewelry. One with a million-dollar price tag. I shall leave the choice to you."

"I'll go look in my safe."

"It has to be an item no robber in the world would pass over."

"I have many such pieces."

"One will do."

"What time shall I expect you?"

"I plan to arrive at your place after supper."

"I have a better plan. Come before, Mr. Lipkin. We can have supper together."

THIRTY-FOUR

Harry Details His Plan over Supper

Mrs. Weinberger's dining room overlooked the ocean. The two large windows were half open. The air was refreshingly and naturally cool. I could see tall sails of boats in the distance and a few people on shore below. The night was quiet and still. I could even hear the sound of waves gnawing sand.

Mrs. Weinberger was standing in front of the table. To one side. Like a waiter in a hundred-dollar-a-head restaurant. Food was laid out like they do for a buffet. Silver dishes. Crystal glass. Folded napkins. Help yourself.

"Since you told me to be discreet," she said, "I have told Mr. Lee to take the evening off."

"Very sensible," I said.

"For tonight, I shall be Mr. Lee."

Mrs. Weinberger gestured to one of the two dining chairs facing each other.

"It's just a light supper," she said. "And my table is one hundred percent kosher."

I sat down.

"Can't beat the real thing."

Mrs. Weinberger gave me a contented smile. Then gave herself one to keep it company.

"We won't stand on ceremony, Mr. Lipkin," she said, handing me a plate. "This is, after all, something of an intimate occasion."

"Whatever you say," I said.

I began digging around. I ended up with some spiced pickled prunes and a blintz. I didn't fancy either. They just happened to be nearest to me. I was never less hungry. The sleepless night. Maria's devotion to her brother and the selfless way she showed it. I couldn't even eat much of the little I took.

Mrs. Weinberger made up for me. She ate all the avocado crunchies, half a baked kosher salami, a lot of the chopped chicken liver, four salmon pancakes, a big spoon of potato salad, two spoons of roasted eggplant salad, and just a little lime Jell-O salad.

"Girls like me," Norma Weinberger said when she was through eating, "we have to watch our waistline."

I looked at it. Her waistline. It was covered by a white full-length sleeveless evening number with a Mandarin collar. The silk was spun through threads of silver outlining willow trees and dragons. A laced slit hem crept down

to her ankles. Apart from her wedding ring, Mrs. Weinberger wasn't wearing jewelry. I wondered why.

"No jewels?" I asked. "I couldn't help noticing."

"I have put everything I have of value in my safe," she
said. "Smart, don't you think so, Mr. Lipkin?"

Not only was it a million miles from smart, it was as
close to being as dumb as you could get. But I didn't say
so. Insults wouldn't change it and there was work to do.

I tried again.

"Mrs. Weinberger. Think of it this way. I'm the thief.
I want to rob you. But you have locked your jewels up
tight."

The lady across the table looked hurt. She'd made
a dumb move. But I couldn't help Mrs. Weinberger's
feelings. Not if I was going to do the job she was paying
me for.

"I didn't think of it like that," she said. "I've been very
foolish."

"It is a mistake anyone can make."

"But I didn't mention what I did," she added quickly.
"About locking my treasures away."

"Are you absolutely certain of that?" I said.

"Not to a soul."

"Not to Mr. Lee? Or Maria? It is very, very important."

"Only to you."

"Then we are still in business," I said.

She gave me a small smile. Like she'd been a real good

girl and finished her homework and brushed her teeth and tidied her room.

I let her smile on for a short while and then pulled her back to the job in hand.

"Did you think about the bait?" I asked.

"Oh, that," she said with a lot of the smile still on view. "I chose an emerald necklace. Mr. Weinberger's last gift. Almost priceless. Will that be sufficient?"

"Just dandy," I said. "Leave it outside your bedroom. On that antique wall table you got under the antique mirror. Leave it like you forgot it. The way you left all the other things that got stolen. My guess is whoever is robbing you goes around when you are asleep and pockets what you forgot to put away."

"And where will you be?" she asked.

"In your bedroom. Where else?"

Her cheeks flushed borscht red. "My bedroom? Why my bedroom?"

"Because you can't get Maria to make me up a bed."

She shifted her voice up an octave.

"Whyever not? I have six guest rooms full of beds. That's what they are there for."

I gave it to her slow and clear.

"Mrs. Weinberger. If Maria makes me up a bed in a guest room everyone will figure I am staying. No thief is going to put on a striped sweater and a black mask and get their swag bag out if they know I'm on the premises. What we have to do is make them think I have gone home. But I will still be here. Undercover. As soon as they bite, I'll be right there. Big bear hunter. Bang. One dead grizzly."

She touched the back of my hand. Briefly.

"That's very brave of you, Mr. Lipkin. Very brave. If it is the gardener, and I am not saying it is, well, Steve is terribly strong. I have seen him chop logs."

"I can handle myself," I said trying hard not to picture Steve with a chopper.

"But my bedroom." Norma Weinberger put her palms to her cheeks. "Really, Mr. Lipkin. I don't know. Honestly. If someone were to discover us. The *shanda*. I would never live it down."

"I won't be actually sleeping in your bed," I said. "Not actually with you. I shall be sitting up all night looking through a gap in the door."

She looked relieved. I would have preferred a look of disappointment. Old men lose their hair. Their teeth. Their patience. But not their vanity. I told myself to stop being a nebbish and carried on with the plan. Same as before. A word at a time.

"Since the whole house knows I am having supper with you we will have to fake my leaving. Make it look like I have driven home. But I'll come back into the house."

Mrs. Weinberger rolled her napkin and pushed it into a silver ring.

"What you are suggesting will not be easy," she said. "Going out and then coming back. It will be almost impossible."

"Why is that?" I asked. "This is a house, not Alcatraz."

My client placed the rolled napkin beside her plate. I was asking her to do something she had never done before. Would never do again. It needed nerve. She was beginning to show some. Her reply was clear and firm.

"Mr. Lee locks all the doors and the main gates and turns on the alarm before he retires. Even on a night off. I don't see how you can leave without Mr. Lee noticing. Even less so reenter."

"I will tell you how," I said. "You get Mr. Lee out of bed. Tell him to fetch my hat. I put on my hat. You say how much you enjoyed our evening together. I say thank you. Mr. Lee lets me out. You wave me good night. I drive to the end of the side road and pull in out of sight. Mr. Lee goes back to bed. You go to bed. Then after ten minutes, by the light of the moon, you slip out of your room, turn off the alarm, open the front door, open the main gate, and I creep back in."

There was a long pause while Norma Weinberger went over it.

"How certain are you that this plan of yours will work?"

she said finally. "I'll be perfectly candid with you Mr. Lipkin, I have my doubts."

"Let me reassure you, Mrs. Weinberger," I said. "For a detective, slipping back after hours is a regular routine."

Her expression moved from total doubt to ninety percent doubt.

"Is that so?" she said.

I pushed it home.

"Sure. It's a caper that runs smooth as a Brooklyn egg cream. I first used it on the Greek kidnap case back in sixty-five. Let myself out through the door and climbed in through the first-story window. I used the tree outside the bedroom. It never fails."

Norma Weinberger's hand once again reached for mine. But this time her touch was firmer. I felt the cold of her wedding ring against my knuckle. I felt a tenderness under her grip. Her gentle grip on old Harry's paper-thin skin covered all over in age stains and raised-up veins.

"I shan't let you down again, putting all my jewels away. So silly of me."

"You will do just fine."

The elderly, dignified, and elegant widow of the late Isaac Weinberger let out a tiny sigh.

"From my heart," she said. "You have my complete trust."

Acid from a pickled prune headed back up my esophagus.

"Something you should know, Mr. Lipkin," she added softly. "My trust. I don't give it often."

"Something I don't get often," I said.

Her tender grasp tightened.

The sky outside had turned indigo. A vast sheet pricked all over with stars. Lights were clearly visible along the highway and in homes dotted around the hills nearby. And there were lights in the cabins of the sailboats and from the beach where people were spending time drinking and eating in the open.

I saw myself looking at another long and sleepless night.

· THIRTY-FIVE ·

Harry Waits in the Dark

While Mrs. Weinberger got herself ready for the night I dragged an easy chair from her lounge and positioned it behind the bedroom door. I pushed the door shut but left a gap of a couple of inches between the frame and the edge of the door with the hinges. That way I would be out of sight but have a clear view of the table and the bracelet.

I sat down and got myself comfortable.

During the furniture shifting Mrs. Weinberger had changed into a silk night robe of the same vintage as her evening dress. Dior's idea of a kimono but without the high collar. She didn't get into bed. She sat on top surrounded by cushions, pillows, and bolsters. She looked like someone prepared for a flood. Or an attack by Apaches.

After a while my client called over.

"Any sign of anyone yet, Mr. Lipkin?"

I put my finger to my lips.

"Mrs. Weinberger. No talking. It will give the game away. The idea is to make out you are alone."

"Sorry, Mr. Lipkin," she more or less whispered. "I am a little scared."

"Try to sleep," I said. "You can't feel scared if you are sleeping."

"I don't feel sleepy."

"Make yourself."

"How?"

"What do you normally do when you can't sleep?"

"I read. After a couple of pages I drop off."

"Then find a book and read. And no more talking."

It was around eleven-thirty when Norma Weinberger turned off the reading light above her bed. It had been the only light in the room. A small soft pool that fell over her shoulders and arms and the paperback in her hands. It was enough for me to work with should I need to. But with the light off and the drapes pulled tight the room was now in total darkness. I couldn't see more than a foot in front of me. I loosened my tie and took off my shoes.

Half an hour dragged by.

A clock somewhere chimed midnight. The moon moved over the house. It shone through the tall windows of the passage leading to the lounge that led to the pool that led to the building beyond where all Mrs. Weinberger's staff, except for Rufus Davenport, spent the night. And it shone on the table and the emeralds. It didn't matter that I was sitting in the Styx. I could see the passage. That was what mattered.

The longer I sat the harder it was to keep from sleeping. The chair was big, soft, and snug. The air of the early hours sweet and soothing. Once or twice I dozed off, waking with a sudden jerky jolt. All shaky and with a dry throat. Now and then I thought I heard a noise. As if someone was walking tiptoe out of range. Or maybe it was the rustle of their clothing. But houses you never slept in before are always full of sounds you can't name. Bats in the attic. Doors not shut tight. Pipes with air in them as well as water.

Shortly after the clock chimed five I got out of my chair and stretched. I could hear Mrs. Weinberger's breathing. It was deep and regular. With just an occasional hint of a snore.

I crossed the room without bumping into anything and made it into the connecting bathroom. Just inside the door I found the light and gave it a tug. A discreet neon bar flickered alive over the sink. I ran cold water from a gold-plated faucet in the shape of a dolphin and threw some over my face. I rinsed out my mouth and turned off the faucet. Then I dried my face with a hand towel and killed the light.

The next move was to go back to my chair. But I didn't make it.

Mrs. Weinberger was standing right in front of me. Her tone was surprisingly calm.

"The necklace is still on the table, Mr. Lipkin," she said.

I stood in silence.

Norma Weinberger moved to the window and pulled open the heavy drapes. Very pale gray light fell into the room. Soft sea-lit light. The kind of gray-white dawn light that comes only when you live close by the ocean. She then crossed the room to her bed and fiddled around with the covers.

"The thief will not come now," she said. "They need the dark. Now there is nothing for a thief to hide in. Is that not so?"

I nodded.

"There are still a few hours for us both to get some much-needed rest before the world wakes," she said. "Do you sleep with one pillow or two?"

"One is plenty," I told her.

"But where will you sleep? I don't recommend the chair."

Norma Weinberger plumped up a pillow and placed it next to hers.

"I'll sleep in my bed," she said. "Unlike the chair, I can thoroughly recommend it."

Then she undid the back of her robe and it slipped gracefully from her body. If she was wearing anything underneath I couldn't see it. In the shadowy half light I saw only Doris Day. With dark hair.

· THIRTY-SIX ·

The Thief Strikes While Harry Sleeps

A woman's voice was calling me.

"Wake up! Mr. Lipkin! Wake up!"

It was the kind of voice I heard waking me eighty-seven years ago.

I was Harry the baby. Opening my eyes to the lace-trimmed drapes of windows filled with the tops of leaf-heavy summer trees and uncluttered skies above the gray roofs of tenement houses. The baby in his cot. The old man on his bed. One journey. One timeless pointless journey.

"Wake up, Mr. Lipkin."

Hands were gripping my shoulders and shaking me. Kind hands with soft skin.

I was half stuck in a dream and half out. Stuck somewhere between. A dream where Amos the chef had built a synagogue out of cheese blintzes. Inside Maria was marrying Steve. Mr. Lee was in a prayer shawl conducting the service. Rufus was in riding boots driving a coach and pair. Somewhere in the center of it all I was struggling to shout something. Where or what I never found out. Mrs. Weinberger had got me unstuck.

"I thought you were dead, Mr. Lipkin," she said. "I've been shaking you. Shaking and shaking."

My eyes did the standard old man's wake up slow focus and settled on Mrs. Weinberger's face. It was so close to mine I could smell cold cream.

"What time is it?" I asked. More out of instinct than curiosity.

She let go of my shoulders.

"I have no idea. Seven. Seven-thirty. Mr. Lipkin, how could it have happened?"

I eased myself slowly upright and shoved the pillow behind my back.

"How could what have happened?"

"The necklace. It has gone!"

It wasn't news I wanted that early in the morning. Or anytime.

Mrs. Weinberger perched herself on the edge of the bed.

"I went to get the necklace to put it back in the safe . . ." she paused. "But the table was empty."

"Not on the floor? Underneath on the carpet? Dropped off maybe?"

She shook her head.

"I looked all over. It was nowhere. Mr. Weinberger's last gift. Stolen."

It didn't take me long to figure out the theft had taken place less than a couple of hours ago. In daylight. Or near daylight.

"Whoever took it must have had some idea of what was going on in here," I said. "They knew I was no longer in the chair and made their move. I got to admit it beats me how."

Norma Weinberger was back in her robe. She looked at me. Helpless. Her fingers fiddled with one another.

"We have missed our one big chance," she said.

"Looks that way," I agreed and scratched an itch around my elbow.

Mrs. Weinberger left a long silence. She was thinking. Thinking deep. I looked at her. A lot closer than I had at any time before. Or had the right. She was my client and you don't stare at your client in that way. But I felt that a night in her bed had given me that right. She was aging. But aging in style. A handsome woman. The hair. The skin. They had better care than a hothouse orchid. I had seen it from day one. But there was something I hadn't seen. A dullness behind her eyes. It made her face waxy. Lifeless. Like the mask they make of the dead. And when she finally spoke her words sounded strangely distant. Disembodied. Like the voice you hear from the loudspeaker on a railway station.

"All that matters Mr. Lipkin, is that you, you know who did it."

I let her carry on.

"During these long days of pain and anguish one thought alone has kept me from sinking into despair. You, Mr. Lipkin. You would discover my thief. And now the time has come. Now you will point the accusing finger and the whole terrible business will be over. They will come and take the robber and put them behind bars. Justice will be done and I shall begin to live my life again in peace and tranquility. And I will owe it all to you."

A private detective gets to hear a lot of speeches they don't expect. I never heard one like this. I didn't know if I should clap or whistle Swanee. I did neither. I noticed the only cover Harry Lipkin had over his bones and gristle was a sheet. I looked for my undershirt. It was on a chair beside the bed.

I reached over and hauled it on.

While I struggled to get my arms and head to poke through the right holes, Norma Weinberger got up from the bed. She moved to the window and thought some more while looking into the early morning sky and the high white scattered duck-down clouds passing over the bay.

Then she turned and faced me. Her expression was nearer the one I was used to. A little dippy on top but bright as a sunrise underneath. The dead look that had taken her was nowhere to be seen.

"What are you going to do now, Mr. Lipkin?" she asked in her normal voice. "What is the next step?"

I'd been doing some thinking of my own.

"We come clean," I told her. "Let Mr. Lee and the others know I was here all night hiding in your bedroom. But say nothing about me dozing off. Let them think I saw it all. The guilty party will be sure to show some kind of reaction. You follow?"

"Perfectly, Mr. Lipkin."

"Tell Mr. Lee to assemble everyone in the lounge."

"Do you have a time in mind?"

"Make it for eleven. I got to get myself organized. Take a shower. Find my socks."

Mrs. Weinberger moved to the bedroom door. Then she turned to face me.

"I almost forgot," she said. "Can I get you breakfast? You must be hungry after such a long night."

I nodded. "Thank you, Mrs. Weinberger."

"Anything special?" she asked.

"I operate best on a plate of eggs. Sunny side up. Two's plenty. Not too burned under. And waffles. I like waffles crisp with honey. And a glass of fresh juice. No special kind. I'm not fussy about juice. Grapefruit juice is good. Any juice is good. Orange. Pineapple. Even carrot. And a cup of coffee. I take coffee black. Not too strong. And one sugar."

I was playing for time. I could have ordered a ten-course meal but it would not have made the slightest difference. The race was over and I was still running.

Mrs. Weinberger made a mental note of my breakfast menu. Then a little of the dead look came back. But only a little.

"Mr. Lipkin. Even I know the thief must be one of my staff."

"Has to be," I said. "Unless you got a ghost living here."

"A ghost?" She laughed. "I never thought of a ghost."

I was counting on it.

THIRTY-SEVEN

Harry Gets Ready

Norma Weinberger served me breakfast and I ate it in bed. It is something I never do. Eat breakfast in bed. I have nothing against the habit. It is just that my bed is in one room and the TV is in another.

After eating half a waffle watching a redhead on TV talking about the weather in Kansas and how it would soon be the same kind of weather in Florida I got out of bed and took a shower. I dried off and got back into my light tan gabardine double breasted. I put on my dark tan mercerized cotton socks, my two-tone brogues, my cream shirt, and my mint-green silk tie. With nothing else to put back on I went and checked myself in the mirror that was on the inside of the closet door. The guy in the reflection looked pretty close to the Harry Lipkin I knew. But he still hadn't a single clue.

"What do you think?" I asked the mug in the mirror.

"Magpies," he grinned. Full of himself. "Magpies stole the stuff."

I laughed. Big laugh. Big sneering laugh.

"Oh, yeah? Since when do birds work nights? Bats work nights. Moths. Owls. Birds sleep nights. And the last time I took a look magpies were birds."

There was a polite tap on the door.

"Hello!" I called out a little startled.

"The butler," a voice announced.

"Come in, Mr. Lee," I said. "The door is not locked."

Mr. Lee came in and looked around.

"Is sir alone?" he asked after a short pause. "I thought I heard voices."

"Me, too," I said. "It is a condition that affects one in fifty. Voices here. Voices there. Medical science is at a loss."

There was a pause. Somewhere near a deep sigh of impatience got stifled.

"We are waiting for you, sir, in the lounge," Mr. Lee said. "In accordance with your instructions."

I followed the butler from the bedroom to the flag-stone path edging the lawn to the room overlooking the pool. The sun was already shining brightly. It was hot. In the low nineties. Someone had opened the flower-colored umbrellas. Beyond the shrubs at the far end of the garden gently moving arcs of sun-dappled water were keeping the lawn from getting thirsty.

Inside they were ready for me to deliver. My audience. Apart from the faint hum of the cooling unit there was absolute silence. It was like when the lights go down in the theater and the curtain goes up. "What now?" No one says it. The silence says it. "What now?" In Ibsen they got an answer.

I looked around.

Maria was closest to me. She was sitting in one easy chair and Rufus in the other. Steve sat alone in the center of the pink velvet sofa and Amos uncomfortably on the piano stool. Mr. Lee stood just to the right of Mrs. Weinberger, who was standing just to the right of me. She was in a pair of drawstring slacks and a loose-fitting cutaway sage shirt with outsize buttons. She stepped out of the group and spoke. And with more authority than I had heard her use before. The voice of the young Norma Weinberger. In the old days. Back in the hat factory. Any problems Isaac couldn't handle, Norma would fix it.

"As you all know," she said, "Mr. Lipkin is the private investigator I have employed to discover why certain items in my possession have gone missing. I use the word 'missing' but it is not strictly correct. They have been stolen. I believe this to be the case and so does Mr. Lipkin, who is a professional in these matters. The items stolen range from an inexpensive porcelain pillbox to a priceless emerald necklace. The necklace was stolen as recently as the early hours of this morning. Someone here is the thief. He or she knows who I am referring to. Now the time has come to reveal the culprit. Mr. Lipkin. If you would be so kind."

She gestured to me to step into the spotlight.

I felt like a cross between a game-show host and the foreman of a jury. But I had nothing to give away and no verdict.

"Thank you, Mrs. Weinberger," I said and stared blankly at her staff.

I had never seen a bunch of people more bewildered. Each one had the same two words written large as a front-of-house movie title over their head. Not Me.

In my pocket was the sheet of paper with the list of suspects and their motives and all the other stuff that I had typed earlier. I took it out and put on my reading glasses. With careful timing and a few long jokes thrown in I could spin out reading it aloud till lunch. During the dessert I might just be able to slip away without being noticed. I cleared my throat and began. Slow and ponderous.

"I have here . . . in my hand . . . a list of names."

It was as far as I got. The doorbell chimed.

It went ding-dong. Like it always did.

"May I be permitted to see who is at the door?" Mr. Lee asked Mrs. Weinberger.

She nodded. I looked to heaven and mumbled words of thanks. Mr. Lee bowed and left the room.

THIRTY-EIGHT

Dr. Glasser Arrives Unexpectedly

The man who rang the bell walked confidently into the room followed by Mr. Lee. He was middle-aged with a full head of closely trimmed silver hair. The pants were linen. Light blue in color. A bleached-out blue. So was the casual jacket. No tie. Deck shoes. No socks. His dark eyes were gentle and his mouth looked like it would smile easy. And turn serious just as easy. He could have been anything. A man with plenty who didn't let it bother him.

"Hi, Aunty Norma," he said cheerily and gave Mrs. Weinberger a peck on her cheek. "What's going on? Some kind of séance?"

He waved a hello to the staff. No one waved back.

"This is my nephew, Rubin," Mrs. Weinberger said. "Harry Lipkin, Dr. Rubin Glasser. Rubin is my sister's son."

"Hello, Mr. Lipkin," Dr. Glasser said and we shook hands.

"Rubin is my doctor, as well as my nephew," she said proudly. "He treats me like a mother. I treat him like a son."

Dr. Glasser smiled at me. Amused and curious.

"What's the game?" he asked. "Maybe I could be in on it?"

"I don't think so, Rubin, dear," Norma Weinberger said. "Mr. Lipkin is a private investigator. A number of thefts have taken place here recently."

Dr. Glasser looked at his aunt. He looked at me.

"What's been stolen?" he asked. "Anything valuable?"

His immediate interest was unexpected. And his question direct. But some people are like that. No ceremony. So I told him.

"All kinds."

Dr. Glasser put his fingers to his chin and used the tips to stroke it. Same as wise old men do when they get to thinking hard about where it all began. And when. And why?

"Could you be more exact about the items?" he said.

"Why?" I asked. "You figure it might matter?"

"It might."

Something in his tone suggested his interest wasn't outside of his work. A doctor's curiosity. Not a nephew's. I gave it a spin.

"Okay, Doc," I said. "A pillbox. Love letters. Jade. You want a full list?"

He shook his head and thought.

"Were they all small, Mr. Lipkin?"

Mrs. Weinberger beat me to it.

"They were very precious to me, Rubin. The love letters more than any other."

"I am sure they were, Aunty," Dr. Glasser soothed. Then he turned to me. "Nothing large?"

"Portable," I said. "Pocket size."

"And you have a suspect?" he asked and turned his gaze on the assembly. "Is that what my aunt's staff is doing here?"

Steve put in. Loud. So everyone could hear nice and clear.

"He's got nothing on nobody. We are clean. All of us. Amos. Maria. Rufus. Mr. Lee. Me. I am telling you, Doc. There isn't an alibi he can bust."

There was a muttering of agreement.

Dr. Glasser dug into his jacket and pulled out a pipe.

Sherlock Holmes smoked one when he wasn't playing the violin or messing around with laudanum.

"Is that true, Mr. Lipkin?" he asked. "No suspects?"

"Kind of," I said.

"Meaning what?" he asked.

I went along with him. Maybe he could lead me someplace I hadn't been.

"Everyone and no one," I said.

He put the pipe back in his jacket. The smoke was going to have to wait.

"Aunty Norma," he said firm but gentle. "We need a few words together. In private."

Dr. Glasser moved close to his aunt. He took her arm and led Mrs. Weinberger to a swing seat by the pool. They sat side by side and the doctor began talking. They were too far away to hear what was being said but it was clear it was plenty. When he was through he waved to Mr. Lee to join them. There was some more out-of-range talking and then the butler returned to the lounge.

He stood in the middle of the room. There was more hubbub from the staff. Mr. Lee put up the palm of a hand to ask for silence. It came at once.

"I have some very important news that affects us all," Mr. Lee said with the detachment of a railway station announcement. "There is no longer any mystery concerning those possessions that Mrs. Weinberger had momentarily considered stolen. Dr. Glasser has solved the case. You may now return to your duties. The matter is closed."

The news had hit me like the first custard pie thrown in a film fight. Slap bang in the face. Dead center. My brain was grappling with the news. It had less success than a mountain climber who lost his rope. Maybe Dr. Glasser knew something I didn't. Maybe they all did. There was no other explanation.

The cook. The maid. The chauffeur. The gardener. They all got up and filed out of the room. And they did so without looking my way. Heads down. Eyes on the floor. I had put them under the white light. Shone it in their eyes. Made them suspects. Made them feel shame.

Mr. Lee came and stood facing me.

"Dr. Glasser has asked if you would be kind enough to wait for him, sir?" he said. "He will not detain you long. Now, if you will permit me, I must attend to my duties. Life has been a little disrupted recently and there is much to put back in order."

Mr. Lee could go. But first I wanted more on Dr. Glasser. More on what he knew and I didn't. I wanted to know just how he could stroll into a room with no socks and a pipe shaped like the saxophone my cousin Bernie played in his high school band and wrap up a caper in minutes I'd got nowhere with in a week. I knew I was just aiming wild but I took a shot anyhow. I had to. It was about pride. Plain and simple. Old and young. It never goes. Same as the bone in your ear. Same size from birth to death. Unchanging.

"Mrs. Weinberger's nephew," I said. "He looks like he's at home here. I guess he drops by quite a bit?"

"Once a week is customary," he replied.

Mr. Lee took a pace to the door. The butler wanted out. I wanted him in.

"Lives close, then?" I said.

"A short drive."

Mr. Lee left a pause.

"Now, sir. If you'll excuse me," he said. "I have a busy morning ahead of me."

I was all through with being treated like a cold kreplach.

"I got a busy morning ahead of me too, bud," I snapped. "I got a busy day. A busy week. A busy life. You will go when I say so."

The man in the white jacket and striped pants froze. Only the Volga in winter froze quicker.

"It is clear Dr. Glasser knows the layout," I said. "He is familiar with what goes on here. Day to day. There is something Dr. Glasser picked up on in minutes that I spent a long week of dead ends looking for. Something you or Steve or Maria or Amos or Rufus forgot to tell me about. Something as important as the law of gravity. You figure you could point me in the direction of that particular something?"

He turned it over.

"As I have previously explained, sir," the butler said, "Dr. Glasser comes here once a week on average. He lives a twenty-minute drive away in West Lake Park. His clinic is in North Miami. As to the suggestion that sir could have been given more information, that is sadly, at least from my point of view, sir, way out of whack."

Mr. Lee bowed and left me standing alone in the room.

That was it. All he had to tell me about Mrs. Weinberger's nephew. His life in three short sentences. How often he dropped by. Where he hung out his washing. Where his patients read *National Geographic.* But there was nothing about his trick. How he discovered so quickly who stole from his aunt. Maybe it stood out like a fresh towel in a three-dollar-a-night motel. Obvious to everyone.

But not to me.

I looked at Dr. Glasser sitting by the pool. He was still heavily in conversation with Mrs. Weinberger. It was all there. The knowing nod of the head. The concerned shrug. The thoughtful folding of the arms. The doctor's way of making you feel that you matter. They learn it along with why blood cells turn white and what to rub on nettle rash. Bedside. Poolside. The manner was the same.

Then I did a bit of diagnosis of my own.

Maybe Mrs. Weinberger had a health problem. It would certainly explain the reason for her nephew's weekly visit. He could hand over her medication and ask how the bridge night went all in one trip. Maybe that was it. Something that Mrs. Weinberger suffered from but didn't show. A little crazy? That was it. Criminally insane. She hired a thief to steal so she could collect the insurance because she lost her savings in a failed business venture and needed the money to pay the bills and . . . Then I called a halt. Enough, Harry, I told myself. This isn't diagnosis. Not even a wild hunch. It is the way an old worn-out and defeated dick tries his best to fight off failure.

The reason would soon be clear. One way or another. Dr. Rubin Glasser was through talking to his aunt and was striding purposefully toward me.

"I am sorry to have kept you waiting, Mr. Lipkin," he said drawing close. "We need to talk in private."

· THIRTY-NINE ·

Harry Learns Mrs. Weinberger's Secret

D r. Rubin Glasser led me along a dark passage I
hadn't seen before. It was on the east wing of Coral
Gables. Where the windows faced the ocean. At the
end of the passage we climbed a narrow flight of stairs
and then walked a short way to an oak-paneled door. It
wasn't locked. Dr. Glasser opened it and ushered me into
the room. He checked that no one had followed us and
closed the door behind him.

"This is just between us," he said. "Understand?"

"Fine by me," I said.

What little light there was came from an oriel window
hidden behind a pair of partly drawn burgundy velvet
drapes. The room was shut tight. It was no bigger than a
cabin on a banana boat and full of junk Mrs. Weinberger
had grown tired of. Some of it was stuff her mother had
grown tired of.

"I could use a little more air in here," Dr. Glasser said. "I can just about breathe. How about you?"

"The more the better," I agreed.

The doctor trod carefully over a pile of hatboxes and pulled back the drapes. Then he pushed at the window. Nothing. He pushed harder. Still nothing.

"I guess it needs a little grease," he said. "Must have been some time since this got opened."

"Want a hand?" I asked.

"I can manage," he said. "It'll shift eventually."

He carried on jerking the handle and I looked around.

Lined up near the door there were six padded dining chairs made in 1876. Round about. Maybe 1877. None had padding. There was a low table that you put a phone at one end and sat at the other. Except you couldn't sit on it because a stack of beaten-up leather suitcases were already sitting there. Hanging on the wall behind the phone chair was half an oval mirror in a peeling hardwood veneer frame. Alongside it was a late nineteenth-century watercolor of Venice. At some point the painting had been exposed to too much damp. Black moldy patches obscured half the Doge's Palace and most of the sky. I would have told people they were storm clouds and kept it on show.

But not everyone thinks like me. Not when it comes to watercolors of Venice.

"Any luck?" I asked.

"Grease would help," he said.

Further inside there was a large silver metal trunk. The kind people take on an ocean liner and cover with travel stickers. In a corner there was a stuffed bear who looked like he would have been more at home in the Yukon jumping on hunters. He was standing upright with a snarling mouth full of yellow teeth and his right front paw missing. The paw was on the floor next to a rolled-up kilim carpet with a label on the back that read "Made in Turkey." And there were cobwebs. Under. On. Between and over. All the room lacked was an uneaten wedding cake and an old lady in a wedding dress wearing one shoe.

Then there was a loud clank. It was the noise a rusted window makes when it opens.

"How's that?" he asked.

A cool breeze wandered in.

"Fine."

Dr. Glasser dusted the top of a tea chest with the word "books" scribbled in capitals on the side and sat down.

"From the discussion I have just had with my aunt," he said, "she employed you to investigate her stolen property?"

He looked at me. I said nothing. I perched on a chair. It was rattan. The sort Van Gogh had in the bedroom of his yellow house. It was the only seat in the room you could sit on.

"'Stolen.' That was the precise word she used?" the doctor said.

"That's about the size of it," I said. "And I guess she used the word 'stolen' because her stuff was there one minute and gone the next. 'Stolen' is the word most people would use."

Dr. Glasser crossed his legs and leaned forward.

"Mr. Lipkin," he said. "What I am about to tell you is strictly confidential. It is not to go beyond these walls. Have I your word on that?"

"Sure," I said. "I'm used to discussing confidences. It's part of my job too."

Dr. Glasser left a short pause. Like he was running through what he was going to tell me. Then he stood up and moved to the console housing a Victrola phonograph which was to the left of the door. Which is probably why I hadn't noticed it. Dr. Glasser looked at the phonograph and then turned to me. Soft. Slow. There was some pain under his eyes.

"My aunt is suffering a degenerative brain condition," he said. "The most common symptoms are a transient loss of memory coupled with general confusion."

I went through the list. Dementia. Alzheimer's. A minor stroke.

"And you figure your aunt's state of mind might have

something to do with people stealing her valuables?" I asked.

Dr. Glasser patted the lid of the phonograph.

"When I was a kid," he said, "I watched my aunt play this machine. She'd sing along with the records. All the big names. Judy Garland. Rosemary Clooney."

"Doris Day?" I said.

He nodded and thought some more. Then he said, "Along with forgetting who is the president of the United States and which day of the week it is, someone suffering from a degenerative brain disease frequently complains that they can't find a familiar object in the place they normally leave it."

The phonograph had a cupboard for storing records. He bent down and pulled at the doors. They were locked. He stood upright again and opened the lid to the turntable. The doctor carried on talking while poking around.

"The examples are all too familiar. 'My watch is not on the night table. I always put it there before I go to bed. I do so regularly. Now it is gone.' The most common conclusion is that the watch has been stolen. Why else would it not be there?"

Very slowly a hazy picture was forming in my mind. An old lady with a fan. Putting the fan someplace. Going back to where she thought it might be. Gone. Stolen.

"You see, Mr. Lipkin," Dr. Glasser continued, "the machinery that we normally use no longer functions.

Reason. Memory. The sense of time. They are all linked. And although they are still in place, like an automobile engine that has no spark, they are quite useless."

Dr. Glasser picked up a small cabinet key beside the turntable and then turned to face me.

"Do you understand yet, Mr. Lipkin, why the word 'stolen' is not appropriate?"

I shrugged.

"I am an old private eye," I said. "I live in a world where thieves only steal from someone else."

The doctor smiled sadly.

"That is true," he said. "But the world we are discussing has another dimension. The thief who steals my valuables knows exactly where to find them. People suffering from neurological impairment put things they believe others have stolen just about anywhere. They stuff them in the back of a closet. Or the back of a drawer."

It was medical knowledge. Outside what I knew. But I got the drift. Dr. Glasser gave me some more.

"Very rarely, a person with this kind of illness puts their so-called stolen belongings in a place that has a strong association with the past. If you can imagine someone who perhaps played a lot of golf, for example. They might easily put them in a golf bag. Do you follow me, Mr. Lipkin?"

The hazy picture suddenly pulled into sharp focus. I looked at the phonograph. At the locked doors.

"And so someone who liked to sing a lot when they were young," I said. "Who liked to sing along with records, someone like Mrs. Weinberger. When they hide something they took from themselves and imagined was stolen, then they hide it—"

Dr. Glasser cut me short. He handed me the key to the phonograph.

"Unlock the doors, Mr. Lipkin."

Everything was there. The pillbox. The love letters. The jade. Stacked in a neat pile. The necklace was on top. Sunlight from the window caught the cut stone. The tiny green beveled edges flickered. Reflecting the light. Like winking stars.

FORTY

Harry Goes Home and Types Out His Report

When I'd gotten back to Warmheart it was raining. More drizzle than rain. But there was some sun that broke through. Weak. Small and distant in a pale gray sky trimmed with blue.

I took a shower. Drank some lemon tea and changed my clothes. Then I sat at my desk. I put a blank sheet of paper in the Remington and typed out the last page of my report. It didn't take long.

Suffering from the early to mid stages of a degenerative brain disorder that causes amnesia and mild paranoia, my client was entirely responsible for the thefts she claimed were the actions of others. All those questioned in relation to the items believed to have been stolen are entirely innocent.

I pulled the paper out of the machine and put it in a folder and put the folder in the filing cabinet. The Weinberger case was closed.

I took the hundred dollar bill I'd been given to solve the case from my billfold and put it in an envelope. I wrote "Amos Moses" on the front care of Mrs. Weinberger's address. Then I sealed the envelope and stuck on a stamp. A hundred bucks might put a few bricks in a wall. If it arrived.

Then I went back to my desk and sat looking at the keys on the typewriter. I sat wondering what happened to the letter *V*? And why the *B* next to it always gets stuck coming back? Little things. Things to take my mind off the big things. Like the case I didn't solve. I kept telling myself that thirty years ago I would have seen it from the start. Medical knowledge or no medical knowledge. Thirty? Twenty maybe. Maybe ten. Five. Last year.

I was fooling myself.

Outside the drizzle had moved on to drizzle over someplace further north. Over at Disneyland kids eating ice cream and talking to Goofy would be getting wet. But my yellow plastic seat in the yard would be nice and dry and the sun of late afternoon pleasantly warm. I went and sat there. And I thought some more about Harry Lipkin.

You are too old for the job, I told myself. A lot too old. Eighty-seven going on eighty-eight. The next time someone calls and says they need a private investigator you tell them find someone else. Someone who can spot auto dementia theft and not make a fool of himself chasing all over town looking for someone else.

And I listened to me talking. I listened carefully. I was making a lot of sense. For the first time in a long time. So I talked some more.

Harry Lipkin. Former private eye. Meet the new Harry Lipkin. A man with time on his hands. You can join the golf club, Harry. Spend an afternoon with other men your age missing a putt from two inches. You can go to bed early. Get up early. Watch daytime TV. All day. Every day. You can buy a baseball hat and gym shoes from the company that got a five-year-old Asian kid to sew them together. And you walk around town all day and show everyone the brand. You can shop ten times a week for special offers and get two for one and pay six cents instead of eight and collect food coupons from super-markets. And Harry. You can finally fix the tiles from the roof you got piled up on the lawn. Mrs. Feldman would be happy to see the tiles fixed and the new Harry Lipkin would be happy to see Mrs. Feldman happy.

I was at peace. But not a lasting peace. It was a peace broken by a distant bell. The bell of the phone in my office. Seven rings. I let it ring. I could just hear my voice in the distance.

"You have reached Harry Lipkin, private investigator.

Leave your name and number and I will call you back as soon as I can."

The caller hung up. No message. As soon as I finished fixing the tiles I'd put on a new message. "You have reached Harry Lipkin. Fun guy. Free anytime."

I sat in the yard until it was dark. I sat thinking back over the years. The early days in a cold automobile staked out on a wet street all night and nothing but a neon sign for company. I thought about cases that got so tough I needed a gun. And I thought about the cases that were so simple I'd solve them before the client got out of the office. I sat thinking a long time. I ended up thinking about the two old Jews living next door. A husband and wife making the best of the worst years of their lives.

I suddenly felt a chill. Not just outside but inside as well. I went back into the office for my jacket. It would keep part of me warm. I had just put it on when the phone rang again.

Let it ring, New Harry Lipkin told Old Harry Lipkin.

But there is no accounting for curiosity. Or habit.

On ring five I picked up the receiver.

The voice began at once. Before I could say a word. It was a woman's voice. Late thirties. Early forties. Sober. White. No accent. Maybe just a hint of somewhere out of town. Out of state. Boston possibly.

"Mr. Lipkin. Oh, Mr. Lipkin," the voice said. "Thank God you are there. I called earlier. I didn't leave a message. I know I should have. But I am not thinking straight. I am desperate. It's my husband. Last night he called from the office and said he would be home late. I waited and I waited. Midnight. One o'clock. All night. Mr. Lipkin, he still hasn't come home. I have this awful feeling—"

"One second," I cut in. "I got to get something to write with."

I picked up a pencil and opened a fresh page in my notebook.

"Okay, lady," I said. "Let me start by taking down a few details." The tiles could wait.

About the Author

Barry Fantoni was the chief contributor and writer for *Private Eye* magazine and a diary cartoonist for the *Times* (London). He is the author of several detective novels published in the 1980s, one of which was published in the United States.